TOP-NOTCH DOCS

These heroes aren't just doctors,
they're life-savers. They fight for those
who don't have the power themselves.

These heroes aren't just surgeons,
they're skilled masters.
Their talent is respected
by colleagues, their reputation
admired by all.

These heroes don't just deal with patients,
they're devoted to their care.
They'll hold the littlest baby in their arms,
and melt the hearts of all who see.

These heroes aren't just medical
professionals, they're warm, charming
and devastatingly handsome.
They're the men of your dreams.

Top-Notch Docs

He's not just the boss, he's the best there is!

Suddenly he was standing way too close.

She looked up into those sea-green eyes and swallowed as she pressed herself even further back against the sink, until her spine protested at the pressure. The atmosphere was so heavy she could even hear the faint dripping of the kitchen tap behind her.

'W-what are you d-doing?' she stammered.

His chest was almost but not quite touching hers. She had only to breathe out fully and her breasts would brush his hard body. She felt as if she was going to drown in the unfathomable depths of his eyes as he leaned in even closer. Her eyelids had fluttered closed, and her mouth opened just a fraction in anticipation of his kiss—when she felt his arm brush past her waist to reach for the tap behind her.

'I was turning off the tap,' he said, stepping back from her. 'What did you think I was doing?'

'I...I...' She floundered for a moment. *The tap? He was turning off the dripping tap?* She could feel her face flaming. Oh, God! She'd been almost begging him to kiss her.

A DOCTOR BEYOND COMPARE

BY
MELANIE MILBURNE

MILLS & BOON®

First published in Great Britain 2006
Large Print edition 2007
Harlequin Mills & Boon Limited,
Eton House, 18-24 Paradise Road,
Richmond, Surrey TW9 1SR

© Melanie Milburne 2006

ISBN-13: 978 0 263 19341 1
ISBN-10:   0 263 19341 1

Set in Times Roman 15¼ on 18¼ pt.
17-0307-59680

Printed and bound in Great Britain
by Antony Rowe Ltd, Chippenham, Wiltshire

Melanie Milburne says: 'I am married to a surgeon, Steve, and have two gorgeous sons, Paul and Phil. I live in Hobart, Tasmania, where I enjoy an active life as a long-distance runner and a nationally ranked top ten Master's swimmer. I also have a Master's Degree in Education, but my children totally turned me off the idea of teaching! When not running or swimming I write, and when I'm not doing all of the above I'm reading. And if someone could invent a way for me to read during a four-kilometre swim I'd be even happier!'

Recent titles by the same author:

Medical Romance™

A SURGEON WORTH WAITING FOR
  24:7
HER PROTECTOR IN ER

Did you know that Melanie also writes for Modern Romance™? Her stories have her trademark drama and passion, with the added promise of sexy Mediterranean heroes and all the glamour of Modern Romance™!

Modern Romance™

THE SECRET BABY BARGAIN
BOUGHT FOR THE MARRIAGE BED
THE GREEK'S BRIDAL BARGAIN
BACK IN HER HUSBAND'S BED
THE GREEK'S CONVENIENT WIFE

To Will and Veronica Turvey
and of course Scamp!
You are such wonderful friends
and we value your friendship so very much.
Thanks for being with us through the
tough times. You are the greatest!

CHAPTER ONE

'Don't even think about it, buddy.' Holly gritted her teeth with determination as the beat-up car behind her tried yet again to edge its way past her on the sinuous stretch of southern New South Wales coastal road.

The car, with a male driver, *of course*, she inserted cynically, had been tailing her since the Baronga Bluff turn-off, edging closer and closer, looking for an opportunity to overtake. The rusty vehicle had clung to her like a barnacle on the back of a boat, taking each tight curve with a roar of its impatient engine, but so far she'd managed to hold him off. She'd stayed just under the speed limit religiously, taking each of the savagely twisted curves with caution but competence.

The winding road began to even out ahead, the window of opportunity obviously not escaping the driver behind her, who once again revved his engine to make a move.

'Put this up your exhaust and smoke it, you idiot,'

Holly said and put her foot down, the surge of two hundred and fifty horsepower instantly coming to her rescue.

However, her victory was very short-lived.

She had to ease back off the throttle when a lumbering farm vehicle turned into the road just ahead of her, its spluttering cough of blue smoke billowing out behind it as it prepared to laboriously climb the steep hill ahead.

Holly allowed herself one short sharp swear word. What was it about male drivers? City and country, they were all the same—arrogantly assuming the road was theirs and theirs alone.

She checked her rear-vision mirror once more and instantly began to seethe.

The driver behind looked like the typical surfing bum—the surfboard strapped to the roof-rack not the only clue. In one or two quick glances she could see he was well tanned with messy, salt-encrusted dark brown hair, the overlong ends bleached naturally by the sun, giving him the sort of highlights she had to sit in a hairdresser's chair for an hour to achieve.

She couldn't see his eyes—they were screened behind one-way sunglasses—but she caught a glimpse of his mouth and her fury ratcheted up another notch.

He was smiling.

The farm vehicle began to choke ahead of her, slowing to an excruciating crawl as she nudged it once or twice from behind.

Because she was tucked so close, the car behind had a much better view of the road ahead and the driver quite clearly knew the route well, for just as she prepared to pull out to check there was a great roar on her right and the old rusty car rocketed past, leaving a trail of exhaust fumes in its wake.

To add insult to injury, the young male driver waved to the older male driver of the farm vehicle as he sped past as if they were old friends.

'Jerk,' Holly muttered under her breath and then, forcibly brushing off her ire, concentrated on the rest of the journey into Baronga Beach, the small south coast town where she'd taken up a position as GP in a two-doctor clinic for a year.

The town was situated on a small bay, the sparkling blue waters coming into view as soon as she crested the last hill. The bay was fringed on one side by rolling hills dotted with cattle and horses, their shiny backs catching the summer afternoon light. She could even smell the sea salt in the air as she drove along the wide main street looking for the address she'd been given.

And there it was.

Baronga Beach Medical Clinic.

How easy was that? No rustling about for street directories or satellite navigation way down here. It was a block from the main drag, a small—by her Sydney standards—nursing-home-cum-medical clinic which served a population of close to fifteen thousand people.

The largest hospital was about two hours away by car, which meant services were somewhat limited but essential to the town's survival. From what she'd read it wasn't exactly a popular tourist spot. The fishing, surfing and diving crowds tended to gather in the more resort type towns further along the highway. There were steep mountains nearby, but by the look of their craggy pinnacles they were not for the faint-hearted in terms of bushwalking.

Holly couldn't help a tiny inward grimace at what she'd impulsively committed herself to. She'd been so keen to leave Sydney after her final GP training posting at the Mosman clinic, she'd taken the first position she'd seen advertised, the country post appealing to her for the very fact that it was exactly what her ex-fiancé would have scathingly described as a hick town.

She mentally chastised herself as Julian

Drayberry's blond and buffed features came to mind. How had she not seen the way their relationship had been wrong from the start? But from now on things were going to be different. What she needed now was space, and Baronga Beach was exactly the place to provide it.

Besides, what better way to heal a broken…no, strike that and replace with slightly cracked heart, she quickly amended, than a stint in a country town where hopefully work would take up every available space so she didn't have to linger on the might-have-beens, could-have-beens, would-have-beens or should-have-beens?

Holly pulled into the clinic car park and found a space next to a colourful bed of bright pink pig's face which was over-spilling its confines. She stepped out of the car and began to edge past the trailing plant when a voice growled at her from a few feet away.

'You can't park there! Get out of that space right this minute!'

She turned to see an elderly man limping towards her, waving a walking stick at her angrily.

'Did you hear me, young lady? This space is reserved for army personnel only. Now move that vehicle immediately or there will be trouble.'

'I'm sorry…' Holly glanced to see if there were any signs she'd missed but there was nothing to suggest she'd parked illegally. She turned back to the elderly gentleman, who was glaring at her from beneath bushy white brows, but before she could think of something to say to quell his obvious ire another voice sounded from the front door of the clinic.

'Dr Saxby? How wonderful to meet you. I'm Karen Pritchard, the receptionist.' A woman of about forty came striding towards Holly and offered her hand. 'Welcome to Baronga Beach Medical Clinic.'

'Er… Thank you,' Holly said with a nervous glance at the old man, who was making slow and considerably unsteady progress towards her.

'Get out of here immediately!' He tapped his stick on the ground for emphasis. 'That's an order!'

'Now, now, Major Dixon, ' Karen, the receptionist, soothed as she took his arm and led him back towards the nursing home annexe of the clinic. 'Isn't it time for afternoon tea? Come on, let's go and see if the mess hall is keeping to its strict time-table.'

Holly watched as Karen handed over the old man's arm to a nurse who had appeared at the door, the amused glances exchanged between the two women speaking volumes.

'Come on, Major,' the nurse said. 'What will Dr

McCarrick say if he hears you've been disobeying his orders? You know he insisted on bedrest until that leg ulcer heals. He'll have you stripped of your medals if you're not careful.'

The old man mumbled something in reply but Holly didn't hear it as Karen came back to her with a welcoming smile on her face. 'Sorry about that. I hope he didn't frighten you. He's one of the nursing home residents.'

'Is he really a major?' Holly asked as she fell into step beside her as they walked towards the clinic.

Karen gave her a sideways grin. 'No, but ever since he developed dementia we go along with it. It keeps him happy. Besides, at nine or ninety, what man doesn't like a bit of power to wield from time to time?'

What man, indeed? Holly silently agreed as she recalled her recent encounter with the driver she'd tussled with on the road into town.

'Well, here is the reception area, Dr Saxby,' Karen said as they entered the building.

'Please call me Holly.'

'Holly, then.' Karen smiled. 'I'm sorry the welcoming committee is a bit thin on the ground but we had an emergency early this morning. I don't think Dr McCarrick is back from the Jandawarra Community Hospital yet. He went in the ambulance with a road accident victim.' She glanced at the clock on the wall. 'He should be back any time soon.'

'That's all right,' Holly said pleasantly. 'I thought I'd just call in to say hello. I have to settle into the house, anyway.' She rummaged in her bag for the address and, unfolding the piece of paper, asked, 'Where exactly is Shelly Drive?'

'It's just a few blocks from here,' Karen informed her. 'It's a lovely little semi-detached cottage. Dr McCarrick lives next door. He bought them both a couple of years ago and completely renovated the one you will be living in; now he's working on the other one.' She handed her a set of house keys and, giving Holly a rueful look, added, 'I hope he doesn't keep you awake at night with all that banging.'

Holly smiled as she took the keys. 'I'm sure I won't even notice. I've just spent three years living in one of Sydney's busiest, noisiest inner suburbs. The sound of traffic and sirens just never stopped, night or day. I think this will be a nice change.'

'It will certainly be a change,' Karen agreed. 'But it's very quiet down here. Most of the action is further along the coast where the tourists head for the better facilities, but I'm sure it won't take you long to settle in. You'll like Dr McCarrick. He's been such a wonderful boost to the local community. He's been single-handedly holding the fort ever since Neville Cooper was forced to retire after a stroke. Cameron will be glad to have another pair of hands to ease the workload. He's been going it alone for too long as it is.'

'I'm sure we'll get along just fine,' Holly said, already mentally conjuring up an image of Dr Cameron McCarrick. She hadn't been told much but she assumed he was the typical country GP—no doubt married with a family, comfortably settled in the community, a bit of a paunch starting from long hours on call, maybe even some hair loss which, if he was anything like her mother's current husband, he would try to hide with the coffee scroll sort of comb-over that always made her giggle behind her polite smile.

Holly was certain they'd get along just fine.

'I could give you a quick tour of the clinic now but you might want to catch the General Store before it closes,' Karen advised with another quick glance at the clock. 'You're probably used to twenty-four hour services but I'm afraid things shut down here at five-thirty on the dot.'

'Thanks,' Holly said. 'I've brought some basics with me but I need milk and fresh fruit.'

'I'll be here at eight so I can show you around then. See you tomorrow,' Karen said. 'Have a good night.'

'I will,' Holly said confidently and made her way outside.

The General Store was still open so she parked her sports car in one of the angled parking spaces and headed inside.

It was nothing like the huge supermarket complexes she was used to, but the food looked reasonably fresh and certainly the freezer compartment was well-stocked. She loaded up her basket with some low-carb, high-protein ready-to-heat meals, snatched up some low-fat milk on the way past, as well as some bananas and locally grown apricots, and made her way to the checkout at the front.

'You new in town?' the checkout girl asked, shifting a wad of chewing gum from one cheek to the other.

'Yes…'

'Nice car,' the girl said, flicking her glance to where Holly had parked. 'You staying long?'

'About a year,' Holly answered.

The girl shifted the gum again. 'You must be the new doctor.'

'I am.'

The girl scanned the items mechanically. 'You

know what you're letting yourself in for living down here?' she asked.

'It looks like a nice place,' Holly offered, not sure what else to say.

'Yeah…' The girl gave her a bored, can't-wait-to-get-out-of-here look. 'You could say that…'

Holly made her way outside to her car and, juggling her groceries on one hip and with her head down against the glare of the hot sun, activated the remote control to unlock the boot.

'Nice car,' a male voice spoke from just beside her.

Holly spun around to see a familiar, scruffy-looking man of about thirty-two or so smiling at her, his eyes shielded behind a pair of one-way sunglasses.

It was *him*.

He was leaning against the old car she'd seen him in earlier, his whole demeanour as he regarded her nothing less than indolent.

Holly fully intended to ignore him but when he pushed himself off the car to step closer she somehow found herself tilting her head to maintain eye contact.

He was a whole lot taller than he'd looked behind the wheel, she thought as she moistened her suddenly gravel-dry lips. And he was extremely good-looking in a casual, just-got-out of the surf or just-out-of-bed sort of way.

She wrenched her gaze away and purposely ran it over his disreputable vehicle in one dismissive glance.

She turned back to look at him and, wrinkling her nose in distaste, returned, 'I wish I could share the same sentiment about your car but I find myself quite without a suitable adjective with which to describe it.'

He tipped back his head and laughed.

It was one of those strong male laughs that sent ripples of reaction to female stomachs if female stomachs weren't adequately prepared.

Unfortunately Holly's stomach hadn't been prepared.

She felt the shockwaves roll through her, even the sensitive hairs on the nape of her neck standing to attention at the rich deep sound.

She tossed her groceries in the boot by way of avoiding that mocking smile, all her hackles rising as she turned back to face him.

'I suppose you think it's funny to play with other people's lives the way you did?' she asked, sending him one of her best full-of-reproach frowns as she closed the boot with a snap.

He took his sunglasses off and cocked one eyebrow at her, the edges of his mouth still curled upwards in what could only be described as a dangerously sexy smile.

'You were hugging the centre of the road,' he said, folding his arms across the expanse of his broad chest.

'I was not!'

'And you were well below the speed limit. You'll get yourself driven over if you do that out here.'

'Like you did to me?' She angled her head at him accusingly, trying not to notice how very attractive his eyes were. They were predominantly blue but had a greenish tinge closer to the pupil which reminded her of the ocean. She was sorely tempted to flick her gaze to the blue-green water of the bay and back for a quick comparison, but somehow resisted the impulse.

'I didn't drive over you,' he said. 'I took the first safe available opportunity to pass you.'

'You were on my tail for miles!' she retorted hotly. 'You almost drove me off the road. I should report you for dangerous driving. You could have caused an accident.'

'I don't think so,' he said. 'I know my way around cars.'

Holly gave his rusty vehicle an ironic glance. 'You call *that* a car?'

He followed the line of her gaze and she heard him sigh as he addressed his car. 'Did you hear that, Bluey?' He stroked the crinkled and mottled bonnet affectionately. 'This young lady just insulted you after all you've done for me today.'

She rolled her eyes and folded her arms across her chest primly. 'Very funny.'

His blue-green eyes met hers, a small smile still playing around the sensual curve of his mouth. 'It's not such a good idea to insult people in a small country town,' he cautioned. 'You never know, it could very well come back to bite you.'

She let her brown eyes run over him slowly, taking in the bottle of Jack Daniels tucked under his arm, his faded board shorts, ragged T-shirt and thong-clad feet, before coming up to the lean line of his jaw, peppered with dark masculine stubble which looked as if it hadn't seen a razor in thirty-six hours at the very least.

'I think I'll take a chance just this once,' she said, straightening her shoulders as she glared at him. 'I've met men like you before. The city I've just left is full of them. Petrol heads without the boost under the bonnet they need.'

His smile was teasing as he creaked open the door of his car, his lazy gaze sliding over her from head to foot, lingering a little too long on the up-thrust of her heaving breasts before he drawled back, 'If ever you want to check under my bonnet to see if I've got the goods, sweetheart, you just let me know. I'd be more than happy to oblige.'

Holly was struck almost speechless at his insolence. How dared he look at her like that, as if he was undressing her with his eyes?

She opened her mouth to flay him but had to turn away with a gasping cough as he began to back out of the space, the choking fumes of his car making her eyes instantly water.

She turned back to mouth an insult at him as he drove away but she was almost certain he didn't see.

He'd already disappeared into a cloud of thick blue smoke.

CHAPTER TWO

HOLLY was so flustered and angry that she took three wrong turns before she finally found the way to the cottage on Shelly Drive.

It was exactly as the receptionist had described: a semi-detached cottage recently and very beautifully renovated, the light blue and white picket fence a perfect complement for the country cream and blue on the house.

The cottage attached was quite clearly still in the process of being restored to some sort of order. As she walked up the pathway to make herself known to her landlord, Holly could see through the uncurtained front windows an array of paint tins and makeshift scaffolding which suggested some major work was still being done inside.

Although there was a four-wheel drive vehicle in the driveway there didn't seem to be the sound of any activity in the house. As she took another quick peep on the way to her front door Holly came to the conclusion that Dr McCarrick couldn't possibly be a family man. No woman in her right mind would consent to live in such a mess.

She knocked on the front door and waited, listening for the sound of footsteps, but no one came to answer her summons.

She could feel the hot sun burning through her linen shirt as she stood on the veranda, tiny beads of perspiration starting to trickle down between her shoulder blades.

After another firm knock and a minute or two of waiting she blew out her breath and, swishing a few loose strands of her hair out of her eyes, made her way to the other cottage.

She unlocked the front door with the key the receptionist had given her and inhaled the not unpleasant smell of fresh paint and recently polished floorboards.

Leaving her bag on a small hall table she looked around with interest. The cottage had been tastefully decorated, the seaside atmosphere highlighted by the white and blue paint theme throughout. Soft billowing curtains hung at the windows, each window fitted with a neat roller blind so that the bright sunlight could be controlled throughout the day.

The kitchen was small but well appointed. She

checked for a microwave and when she finally found it behind a clever cupboard door, gave an audible sigh of relief. Cooking had never been one of her strong points and her busy time at medical school and her internship at the Royal North Shore Hospital had meant the only type of cuisine she was comfortable preparing was of the heat-and-serve variety.

The one and only bedroom was again not large but it had a wall of built-in cupboards which made it seem more spacious. The bed was a small double, but she was well used to sleeping alone and couldn't see that changing any time in the near future.

Her experience with Julian Drayberry had taught her well. She was going to concentrate on her career for a change. Besides, if what she'd seen so far was any indication, Baronga Beach was hardly likely to turn up anything other than geriatric men with attitudes and surfing hippies who had nothing better to do than run other people off the road.

She was on her final trip out to her car to get the last of her things when she heard the sound of a car turning the corner at the end of the street. She looked up to see the now all-too-familiar beat-up vehicle rattling along until it finally came to a hacking cough stop in front of a dilapidated house a couple of doors away.

Holly drew in a tight little breath as she watched

the driver unfold himself from the car, and gave a mental grimace as she reached for her suitcase. Wasn't it just her luck that Mr Surf Bum was going to be a neighbour? She knew there weren't a whole lot of streets to choose from in Baronga Beach, but why did it have to be *her* one that he resided in?

She hoisted the bag out of the boot but one of the straps got stuck on the way past. She gave it a tug but it wouldn't budge.

'Need a hand?' The same lazy drawl assaulted her ears for the second time that day.

Sending her eyes on a roll heavenwards, she stiffened her shoulders and, turning her head, gave him an overly sweet smile which did very little to disguise her gritted teeth. 'Actually, I'm doing just fine,' she said and gave the bag another almighty tug.

The bag sailed out and landed at her feet with a loud explosion as the catch snapped open, spewing clothes and shoes in all directions.

Holly looked down at her open suitcase. All her neatly folded clothes were now sprawled over the driveway and, to her absolute horror, the cheeky going away present the girls from the Mosman clinic had given her had rolled out of its brown paper wrapping and was now busily buzzing enthusiastically at the man's thong-clad feet.

Holly wanted to die.

'Wow,' the man said as he bent to pick it up and began turning it over in his hands. 'I've always wanted to see one of these. How does it work?'

Holly gave him a how-the-hell-would-I-know? sort of look but it was clear he didn't buy it.

'What's this button for?' He pressed it before she could think of something to say and her face flamed anew as a pre-recorded husky male voice said something erotically suggestive.

'Give me that!' She snatched it out of his hands and, fumbling for a moment, finally managed to find the off switch.

She could feel his amusement coming towards her in waves as she stuffed the offensive object in amongst what was still left in her bag, her cheeks so hot she was sure she was going to be incinerated on the spot.

'Here, let me give you a hand,' the man offered helpfully, bending down to retrieve some of her underwear.

If anyone had told Holly she wouldn't be totally mortified by a perfect stranger picking up her bright pink knickers off the pavement even an hour ago she would have laughed, but the truth was—after the previous incident—her lingerie collection didn't even rate a score on the embarrassment scale.

'Thank you,' she said stiffly and took the tiny garment from him.

'It looks like you might need a new bag,' he observed, handing her a lacy black bra.

She did her best not to notice the way his eyes crinkled up at the corners as she took it from him but it was hard going. He had the most expressive eyes she had ever seen on a man, maybe even on anyone.

'Yes…' She stuffed the rest of her clothes haphazardly in the bag and once it was done, straightened and, giving him a smile that lacked sincerity, said, 'Thank you for your help. I wouldn't want to keep you from whatever it is you are doing.'

'As it happens I'm not doing anything right now, so if you need a hand settling in I'd be happy to hang around.'

'No, thank you,' she said, elevating her chin another fraction. 'I think I'll wait until my landlord arrives. No doubt he will want to show me around himself.'

There was a funny little silence.

'Have you been introduced to him yet?' he asked.

Holly wasn't sure what to make of his unreadable little smile. It made her wonder what exactly Dr McCarrick was like. Karen Pritchard, the receptionist, had spoken highly of him but then she was a middle-aged woman who might not have the same critical judgement.

'No...I haven't yet had that privilege,' she answered. 'Do you know him well?'

'Pretty well, I guess.' He rocked back on his heels and whistled through his teeth for a moment as he looked down at her. 'So, I take it you're the new doctor?'

Holly couldn't resist an imperious look at him down the length of her nose. 'Yes, that's correct.'

He didn't look all that impressed, she noted somewhat resentfully.

'Where are you from?'

'Sydney.'

'What part?'

'The northern suburbs,' she answered with a hint of North Shore pride.

'A city girl, then.'

Holly tightened her mouth without responding. The way he said it made it sound as if it was something to be ashamed of. Her ire towards him went up another measure. What was it with him? As far as attitudes went he took the cake and the icing and candles, too.

'So, how long are you down here?' he asked.

'The locum is for a year,' she informed him. 'But apparently after a year I have the option of staying on if I find things to my liking.'

'If you have a thing for one in two on call and everyone knowing your business then you'll settle in well,' he said. 'This is a small country seaside town and nothing, and I mean nothing, escapes the notice of its residents. Sure you can handle that?'

Holly straightened her spine. 'Of course.'

He gave her a lengthy look and added, 'There are no nightclubs and cinemas here and the only restaurant is a Chinese one run by a retired farmer, but let me tell you it's not quite Chinatown.' His eyes twinkled as he added, 'It's known locally as Hoo Flung Dung.'

In spite of her irritation towards him, Holly found it hard not to smile. He certainly had a sense of humour, even if it wasn't exactly to her taste. She schooled her mouth back into a thin tight line and informed him curtly, 'I'm here to work. I'm not interested in anything else.'

His blue-green eyes flicked to her suitcase for a moment before returning to hers. 'I take it there's no current boyfriend?'

Holly dearly wished she could invent one on the spot. How wonderful would it be to have a man appear at her side to dispel his assumptions about her right here and now?

'I hardly see that it's any of your business,' she said some-what tartly.

He gave her one of his stomach-tilting smiles. 'At least you've come here well prepared.' His twinkling eyes went to her bag and back to her still flaming cheeks. 'Wise of you.'

Holly decided it would be better to gather up what remained of her pride and get away from his hateful presence before she made an even bigger fool of herself. She bent down and snapped her bag shut, and with a strength she had no idea she possessed, hauled it to the front door, praying earnestly that the buckle would hold until she was safely inside.

'See you around,' the man called out cheerily.

Holly gave him one last chilly look and shut the door with a definitive snap.

Holly arrived at the clinic an hour early so she could familiarise herself with her new surroundings.

She'd spent a quiet night in her new rented home, her ears pricked for any sound from the cottage next door, but apparently Dr McCarrick had either not come home for the night or he was much quieter than Karen Pritchard had described.

Karen greeted her when she arrived and began to show her around the facilities. 'The bathroom is down there and here is the tea room,' she said as she opened the door of a tiny room.

Holly peered past the receptionist, trying not to think of the plush suite of rooms she'd left in Mosman, with its cappuccino maker and leather armchairs and sofa in the doctors' room.

Baronga Beach Medical Clinic ran to an old kettle, a few mismatched chipped mugs and a fridge that was making some very strange noises against the far wall. There was a small table and four chairs but none of them looked particularly comfortable.

'Of course it's probably nothing like you're used to.' Karen voiced Holly's thoughts out loud. 'But it serves the purpose. Besides, some days we're lucky if we even get a tea break around here.'

She closed the door and led the way to the consulting rooms and, opening the first door, informed Holly, 'This is Dr McCarrick's room. It's a bit bigger than yours but then he is the senior GP.'

Holly gave the room a quick assessing glance. There was a large desk with a computer positioned to one side of it, a bookcase which was jampacked with books and journals in rather a haphazard manner, suggesting the doctor wasn't the tidiest of persons. There was a scattered pile of newspapers on the floor near the desk and a pot plant that looked as if it was in great need of water.

'He doesn't like us to tidy up in here,' Karen explained. 'He says he can't find anything after we've been in. Every few months or so he has a big clean up but in a matter of days it's always back to square one.'

'So what's the arrangement with the treatment room?' Holly asked. 'Do we take turns or something?'

Karen shook her head. 'No, just give him a buzz on the intercom to check if it's free. Now, come this way and I'll show you your room.'

The room she'd been assigned was again nothing like the one she'd used in Sydney but it had the basics for all that. There was a desk and chair, a small bookcase and an examination table and equipment trolley beside it. There was a single window which looked out over the rear end of the nursing home section of the hospital.

Holly turned around to face Karen and gave her a wavering smile. 'It's very…nice.'

'Yeah, well, it's not exactly Macquarie Street in Sydney but hopefully you'll soon feel right at home. I'd better show you the treatment room and the store before the patients start arriving.' There was the sound of a bell at the reception desk and she closed her eyes and grimaced. 'That will be old Mrs Erma Shaw. She comes to all of her appointments at least half an hour early. It drives Sally, the other part-time receptionist, and I crazy at times. She talks non-stop and it's impossible to get away from her.'

Holly gave an understanding smile. 'I had at least five patients like that in the last practice I was in.'

'Just as well then, as it's you she booked in to see,' Karen said as she opened the treatment room door. 'I think you'll be getting the once-over by most of the town over the next few days.'

The treatment room was well equipped with emergency equipment and a locked drug cupboard as well as the usual open-drawer trolleys with bandages and dressings. There was a strong light for minor surgical procedures suspended from the ceiling over a very basic procedure table, and there was resuscitation equipment on hand.

'I think you'll find everything you need in here but if there's anything else you'd like us to stock just let us know.' Karen led the way out again. 'By the way, did you get to meet Dr McCarrick yesterday?'

'No,' Holly answered. 'I was watching out for him but he didn't appear to come home, although I think it was his car in the driveway.'

'That's because he was probably staying with a neighbour a couple of doors down. He did that a lot when he was renovating your place. He mustn't have finished his bathroom yet.'

'Speaking of neighbours, I met one of them yesterday.'

'Oh?' Karen gave her an interested look. 'Which one?'

'He didn't get around to telling me his name, but I can tell you I wasn't all that impressed with either his appearance or his attitude.'

'That would have been Harry Winston,' Karen said. 'He's more or less considered a bit of a no-hoper around here but Dr McCarrick always makes an effort to spend some time with him. He likes a drink now and again but he's really pretty harmless. He's not a mean drunk, if you know what I mean.'

Holly wasn't exactly in agreement on the harmless tag. 'He nearly ran me off the road as I came into town,' she informed the receptionist darkly.

Karen looked shocked. 'Oh, no! Don't tell me he's driving again. He had his licence disqualified three months ago for DUI. Dr McCarrick will be so disappointed; he's been really trying to help Harry get sorted out since he was arrested.'

'*Arrested?*' Holly stared at the older woman, her heart beginning to thud in alarm. 'What for?'

The receptionist shrugged casually. 'It was basically a trumped up assault charge—a pub fight that got out of hand. The charges were dropped before it went to trial, thank God.'

Holly couldn't quite disguise a convulsive

swallow. She knew a little too much about the legal system and what it could do to people. Her cousin Aaron was currently serving time for a crime he couldn't even remember committing. A combination of alcohol and recreational drugs had seen him face an indefensible assault charge. His young life was ruined by a mistake that should never have happened and wouldn't have happened if he'd been a little more careful in his choice of friends.

'Don't look so worried,' Karen said. 'Harry Winston's not the one to be frightened of around here.'

'Oh?'

Karen gave her a conspiratorial look and lowered her voice to an undertone. 'As of three days ago Baronga Beach now has a murderer living on the outskirts of town.'

Holly stepped backwards in shock. '*A murderer?*'

Karen nodded grimly. 'Noel Maynard served twenty-five years for the murder of a local teenage girl. He's just been released out on parole. No one is happy about it, of course, but what can you do? The prison psychiatrist has given him the all-clear and apparently he's been a model prisoner so he was let out. He's staying out on a property in the hills with his elderly mother. Of course, she's always claimed he didn't do it but then that's part of being a mother, I guess. No one wants to think their child is capable of such a vicious crime. '

'Yes…I suppose so…' Holly frowned at the irony of it all. She'd thought by coming to a quiet country town she'd be well out of the way of the underbelly of crime that made working and living in inner Sydney so terrifying at times, never thinking she'd be rubbing shoulders with convicted criminals.

'Tina Shoreham was my best friend,' Karen said into the little silence, her expression immeasurably sad. 'Not a day goes past that I don't think of all she missed out on because of that creep. He cut her life short. Strangled her with his bare hands and stabbed her and left her to the crows to…' She stopped and dabbed at her eyes for a moment before she continued. 'Her parents, Grant and Lisa, have no other children, so there are no grandchildren to look forward to, no birthdays to celebrate—just raw, painful, relentless grief and anger at what Noel Maynard did.'

Holly was uncomfortable with the older woman's emotions on a subject that was obviously still very painful for her. What could anyone say to relieve that level of grief and suffering?

Karen began to lead the way back to reception. 'So you see, Harry is nothing to worry about at all.

Besides, he's too old to get up to too much mischief these days.'

'Old?' She stopped in her tracks to stare at the receptionist.

Karen swivelled around to look at her. 'What, you didn't think he looked old?'

'No...' Holly frowned as she brought the man's scruffy but undeniably handsome features to mind. 'Well, at least not much more than his early thirties.'

'You must have caught him on one of his good days, then,' Karen said. 'When he remembers to shave he can actually look quite presentable.' She gave a little chuckle and added, 'That car of his, however, is another story.'

Holly's mouth tightened. 'His car—and I use that term very loosely—didn't look roadworthy and certainly didn't sound it. I had a few words with him but he was incredibly insulting.'

Karen frowned. 'Oh, dear, that doesn't sound like Harry at all. He must have been having a very bad day. I'll mention it to Dr McCarrick when he comes in. He should be here shortly. Why don't you make a start since you're here early? Erma will be busting a gut to be the first patient to see the new doctor in town.'

A few minutes later Holly was sitting opposite the elderly Mrs Shaw, who had not drawn breath for the last ten minutes. She had given Holly a run-down on the town's history, including that of her great-great-great-grandfather's role in settling the town in the height of the timber-felling era.

'It was tough in those days, Dr Saxby,' Erma said. 'No place for a woman. Of course, someone like you wouldn't have lasted a day or two at the most.'

Holly straightened in her seat. 'What do you mean?'

Erma gave her a look from beneath beetling brows. 'You're a city girl, they tell me.'

'Um…yes…that's correct.'

'This is a rough sort of place for a city girl,' the old woman said. 'There aren't any creature comforts this far down the coast.'

'I'm sure I'll manage to survive,' Holly put in.

The old woman leaned forward on her chair, her beady eyes very intent. 'I suppose you've heard about Noel Maynard?'

Holly opened her mouth to answer but Erma was already continuing in the same cautionary tone. 'He killed once and he'll kill again. Don't have anything to do with him. He's not to be trusted, especially around helpless young women. Let Dr McCarrick deal with him.'

Holly wasn't too happy about being automatically assigned a helpless female role although she wasn't entirely sure she wanted a convicted murderer on her patient list, either.

'Are you married?' Erma asked before she could think of a suitable response.

'Er…no…'

'Boyfriend?'

Holly hoped her cheeks weren't showing the heat she could feel from the inside. 'No…not at present.'

'You won't find one down here,' Erma told her. 'Not unless you take a fancy to the doctor, but let me tell you, he doesn't have much time for city girls after what happened before.'

Holly found herself leaning forward on her chair, her voice automatically lowering in response to her rising intrigue. 'What happened before?'

Erma pursed her lips for a moment as if considering whether or not to tell her. 'It was a nasty business.'

'It…it was?'

'Oh, yes.' Erma nodded gravely. 'They were practically walking up the aisle when she ran off with another man.'

Holly's stomach caved inwards in empathy. Hadn't she had the very same thing happen to her just a matter of weeks ago?

'Oh…that's awful…'

'Too right, it was, and he took months to get over it,' Erma informed her conspiratorially.

'Is he…OK now?'

Erma sat back in her chair. 'He's making some ground but we all keep a close watch on him. He's really rather special to us all. We wouldn't want to lose him.'

Holly gave a mental gulp. What was Erma suggesting? That Dr McCarrick was somehow suicidal?

Oh, what had she committed herself to?

'Mind you, he could do with some help around here,' Erma went on. 'I hope you're going to carry your weight, young lady, as he's been running this town single-handedly for far too long.'

'I am more than prepared to do my fair share,' Holly said firmly. 'Now, since you're here to see me, is there anything I can do for you today? I've checked through your notes and it seems you've not long recovered from a cut on your leg which Dr McCarrick sutured for you. How is it going?'

She was immensely relieved when the old woman lifted her skirt to show her the purplish scar on her leg. This was the sort of stuff she was trained to deal with, not intimate disclosures about the man she was going to be working alongside for the next twelve months!

CHAPTER THREE

HOLLY looked up at the clock at lunch time and wondered where the morning had gone. She still hadn't met Dr McCarrick but Karen had informed her he'd been called out for a home visit which had meant the rest of his patients had to be transferred to her instead.

Holly had been more than pleased to help and had quite enjoyed working her way through the appointments, some of which had been quite challenging, but she felt pleased she'd been able to handle them with increasing confidence.

Once the last patient of the morning had left she stretched out her legs beneath the desk and sighed. There was a quick rap at the door but, before she could tell whoever it was to come in, the door opened and a man stepped into her consulting room.

It was *him*!

He had showered and shaved and his sea salt-encrusted hair was now shiny and clean and neatly styled. And instead of his well-worn and faded board shorts he was wearing clean blue jeans and an open-necked cotton shirt which highlighted his tan and made his eyes—this time—seem even more green than blue.

Holly got stiffly to her feet and cast him a reprimanding look. 'I'm afraid you have missed the morning's consultation clinic. You'll have to rebook for this afternoon's session unless it's an urgent matter.'

'It's not urgent, but I thought I should make myself known to you,' he said with a smile lurking at the edges of his mouth.

'I already know who you are,' she said through tight lips. 'Now, I suggest you leave my office and make a proper appointment with the receptionist.'

He sauntered across the room to stand in front of her desk. 'I don't have to make an appointment. I usually come and go as I please.'

Holly's hands gripped the edge of the desk as she raised one finely arched brow imperiously. 'You will have to do so in future if you wish to see me.'

His blue-green eyes glinted as he looked down at her. 'I thought you might make an exception for me. After all, we're going to be neighbours.'

'Look Mr...er, Winston—' Holly perfected her

best schoolmistress tone '—I've had a busy morning and I do not appreciate you barging in here without a proper appoint—'

'McCarrick.'

'—ment because it's not fair on the other patients who have to wait to see either me or Dr Mc—' She blinked at him for a moment as his smile widened.

'Cameron McCarrick,' he said, offering her a hand. 'Dr Cameron McCarrick.'

Holly gulped and gasped simultaneously. 'You're…*you're Dr McCarrick*?'

He inclined his head, his eyes dancing with obvious amusement. 'Howdy pardner,' he drawled. 'Welcome to Baronga Beach Medical Clinic.'

For once, the years of clinical training she'd endured didn't come to Holly's rescue. Her quick-flash temper completely overrode her usual professional calm and iron-clad control. Her eyes flashed indignant fire at him as she stood almost shaking with rage at the way he'd deliberately misled her about his true identity.

'You b-b—jerk!' she spluttered.

He raised his brows slightly. 'Not quite the greeting I was expecting from a smart city girl.'

'It's the greeting you deserve!' she shot back. 'You deliberately misled me. You damn well knew who I was from the word go and yet you played me for a fool every chance you could.'

He folded his arms across the broad expanse of his chest as if preparing to wait out a childish tirade, which only goaded her into further incautious speech.

'How dare you let me think you were a surfing layabout? Not to mention driving that ridiculous car and pretending to be one of the neighbours. You had numerous opportunities to set me straight, but no— you were waiting until I'd dug a hole big enough to bury myself in so you could have the biggest laugh at my expense. Men like you make me sick. You think you're so smart but, let me tell you, I know how to handle jerks like you.' She stopped for breath, her chest still heaving.

'Are you done?' he asked with implacable calm.

'No, I am not done!' She thumped her hand on the desk for emphasis. 'I've got a good mind to report you. No wonder country towns have such trouble attracting competent medical personnel if this is the treatment they receive on arrival. What exactly is your motive? Or is this your idea of entertainment in lieu of a cinema or whatever else this town lacks?'

'What this town lacks is a sense of humour in its new female doctor,' he said with a touch of dryness.

Holly let out a gasp of outrage. 'I can't believe men

like you still exist. Just exactly where do you get off? I have a sense of humour but I'm afraid it doesn't quite stretch to appreciating puerile practical jokes that at worst belong in a middle school playground, not at a medical clinic.'

'You were the one to make the all-too-ready assumption that I was someone else,' he pointed out.

'How could I not make that assumption? You were driving like a maniac, you had a bottle of Jack Daniels under one arm and you were dressed like a homeless person. You didn't look anything like a responsible country GP.'

'I was driving a mate's car back to town as I'd gone to Jandawarra in the ambulance with a patient. I admit Harry's car isn't exactly *Wheels* magazine car of the year, but it got me back where I needed to be. Besides, I was doing him a favour returning it to him. It's been impounded for months.'

'For drink-driving, I believe?' She sent him a scathing look. 'You know what they say about hanging around with convicted criminals; if you hang around stray dogs, sooner or later you'll pick up fleas.'

He shook his head, communicating his disdain. 'Typical. You city girls are all the same. Appearances are everything. If a guy isn't wearing the right clothes or has the right hairstyle or driving the right sort of car or mixing with the right sort of people. Then…' he gave his fingers a snap '…you move on to the next guy who might be closer to fulfilling your unrealistic expectations.'

'Like your ex-fiancée did?' Holly said before she could stop herself.

The green went out of his eyes to be replaced by a steely blue. 'I hardly think that is any of your business, Dr Saxby.'

It was too late to take the words back but Holly was too angry to apologise. She decided some time out was probably the best way to go so, with a toss of her head, she made to brush past him. 'Excuse me, I'm going to have some lunch.'

A long, tanned, very strong arm suddenly blocked her path, the contracted muscles against her stomach communicating their strength through the thin raw silk of her blouse. Holly sucked in her stomach and dragged her eyes up to the glittering hardness of his.

'If we are to work in any sort of professional harmony, Dr Saxby, I would suggest you refrain in future from mentioning anything whatsoever to do with my personal life. Is that understood?'

Holly gritted her teeth. 'I would suggest, Dr

McCarrick, that you take away your arm before I forcibly remove it. Understood?'

It annoyed her that he smiled. It really, *really* annoyed her. The brief flare of anger in his eyes had disappeared, to be replaced by a twinkling amusement which she could only assume was his usual response to every situation. Holly knew she had a tendency to take life a little too seriously at times, but she resented him stringing her along when at any point he could have introduced himself properly. She didn't like being laughed at, nor did she like being on the receiving end of a practical joke which had made her seem both foolish and prejudiced. What did he hope to gain from it? She was already feeling a little out of her depth as it was, and having him play the clown all the time was not going to make her feel any more comfortable, especially as she would have to work so closely with him.

She gave him another warning glare and after a few beats of holding her gaze he removed his arm and stepped aside, his mouth still tilted in obvious amusement. She threw him a fulminating look as she stalked past, only just resisting the temptation to slam the door as she left.

Karen was in the tea room when she came in. 'I've just boiled the kettle. How do you have your tea?' She stopped mid-pour when she saw the expression on Holly's face. 'Is something wrong?'

Holly folded her arms across her chest. 'I just met Dr McCarrick.'

'Finally,' Karen grunted. 'Poor darling's been run off his feet this morning. I don't know how he does it, really I don't. A lot of doctors these days refuse to do house calls—too time consuming—but he never says no. He's an angel. There's just no one like him.'

Holly inwardly seethed. 'No, I'm sure there's not.'

Karen handed her a cup and pushed the milk and sugar closer. 'There are sandwiches under that tea towel. The nursing home kitchen staff send them each day but if you'd like something else there's a milk bar two blocks away.'

'No, this will be fine... I'm not all that hungry, anyway.'

Karen gave an empathetic sigh. 'First-day nerves. Don't worry, you'll be fine. We're really like one big happy family here, aren't we, Cameron?' she asked as he came in at that moment.

He gave the receptionist a quick grin and reached for a sandwich. 'That's right, Karen. One big happy family.'

Holly felt like rolling her eyes. She felt the weight of Cameron's blue-green gaze as she nibbled ineffectually at a triangle of ham sandwich and, turning her head the other way, caught the tail end of Karen's speculative look.

'You don't seem to be enjoying that sandwich, Holly.' She passed the plate of sandwiches across. 'Have one of the egg ones, they're quite nice.'

She took one to be polite. 'Thank you.'

Cameron took the chair opposite and reached for another sandwich with one hand and the newspaper with the other. He took a bite of the sandwich and, flicking the paper to straighten it, leaned back in his chair, one ankle crossed casually over his muscled thigh.

The phone rang in reception and Karen bustled off to answer it. Holly listened to the occasional rustle of the newspaper and the protest of the chair when he leaned forward for another sandwich but she stalwartly refused to engage in idle chit-chat with him.

Angel, indeed! She silently fumed. He was probably laughing at her right now behind that damned newspaper.

'What star sign are you?' he asked.

'Excuse me?'

He lowered the paper to look at her. 'Let me guess... Scorpio, am I right?'

This time she did roll her eyes. 'No.'

'Virgo?'

'No.'

'Then what?'

She gave him an I'm-a-scientist-and-above-all-that-nonsense look. 'You surely don't believe in that stuff?'

'I don't know; there could be something in it.' He flicked the paper once more and bent forward to read. 'Listen to mine. "With the cosmic upheaval currently going on around you just now you should take extra care when dealing with difficult people who will not appreciate your quirky sense of humour."' He looked at her over the paper again and grinned. 'Pretty accurate, huh?'

She gave him a withering look. 'Does it also say you should act your age instead of your shoe size?'

His smile widened disarmingly. 'You really are uptight, aren't you? Are you sure you're not a Virgo?'

'I suppose you could be nothing but a Gemini with your propensity to switch identities,' she tossed back.

'Wow, I'm impressed!' He reached for another sandwich and took a generous bite and started to chew.

A full minute passed in silence.

'What do you mean I'm uptight?' Holly glared at him.

Cameron took another sandwich and peeled back the thin slice of bread to inspect the contents before answering. 'This isn't the big, bad old city, Holly. Everyone knows everyone around here. We don't stand on ceremony. Your patients will not just be your patients, they will become your friends. And, as for your medical partner...' he gave her another cheeky grin '...I'm not just your colleague but your landlord and neighbour as well.'

She sent him a challenging look. 'I can always find somewhere else to live.'

'You can, but you won't come up with anything remotely like you're used to.'

'How do you know what I'm used to?'

His blue-green gaze swept over her, taking in her Lisa Ho skirt and blouse and Garry Castles sandals. He lingered over her lip-glossed mouth for a moment before roving over her subtle but expertly applied make-up and smoothly blow-dried shoulder-length honey-brown hair with its meticulously spaced blonde highlights.

He rocked back in his chair so it was perched on two legs as his eyes came back to hers. 'If there's an emergency out here you won't have time to put your face on. I expect you to be ready instantly, not dawdling about choosing which outfit to wear.'

Holly stiffened in anger. 'I know how to respond to an emergency.'

'Are you EMST trained?'

She shifted in her seat uncomfortably. Her sudden break-up with Julian had completely thrown her the weekend she'd attended the course in Adelaide. She'd failed the final practical and, to her shame, she had been the only one of the sixteen candidates to do so. She had been meaning to resit the practical exam but hadn't so far garnered up the courage.

'Yes…I mean no…' She lowered her gaze a fraction. 'I have to resit the practical.'

'As soon as you get the opportunity you should do so,' he said. 'Too many lives are lost in remote regions because of inadequately trained medicos who don't know how to assess and treat severe injuries in proper priority.'

'I know… I just haven't had the time…'

'Make the time.' An edge had crept into his tone that she'd not heard before. 'I want to be able to rely on you to back me up in an acute situation. I don't want you panicking and doing the whole flustered female thing. We are responsible for thousands of lives way down here and I need to know I can rely on you at all times and under all circumstances.'

Holly was still boiling at the whole 'flustered female thing' and wondering how best to respond to it when Karen came bursting through the door.

'Kelly Springton's husband just called. Kelly's gone into labour. He's bringing her in. I've called the Jandawarra ambulance but from the sound of it they're not going to make it in time.'

Cameron was on his feet, his short sharp expletive slicing the air like a scalpel. 'We can't let her lose this one. Come on.'

Holly followed him out of the room, her heartbeat starting to escalate in time with her hurried footsteps. 'What happened before?'

Cameron gave her a grim look as he shouldered open the doors connecting the consulting rooms with the small six bed hospital section of the complex. 'She went into labour out on their property when the roads were cut by floods about eighteen months ago. By the time I got there with the help of the State Emergency Service the baby was stillborn.'

'Oh, dear...'

There was the sound of squealing brakes as a car took the turn into the hospital.

'You ever delivered a baby before?' he asked as the doors swung shut behind them.

'Once or twice but the obstetrician was there as well.'

He didn't answer but Holly could see that for once his eyes were not smiling. There was tension in his jaw and in his tall body as he strode towards the Springtons' car as it came to a screeching halt in front of them.

CHAPTER FOUR

HOLLY watched as the young woman was placed on a trolley and wheeled into the examination cubicle, her distraught husband by her side.

'Hold on there, Kelly.' Cameron gave the young woman a gentle pat on the leg as the nurse on duty pulled the curtains around the cubicle. 'You're in safe hands. Just try and breathe through each contraction while I take a look. Try not to worry, Tony—' he did his best to reassure the hovering, white-faced husband as he examined Kelly '—you got her here, that's the main thing.'

He turned to the nurse on duty. 'The head is on show. Get me sterile gloves and an instrument pack, plenty of clean linen and the IV trolley.'

'But we can't deliver a baby here; this isn't a maternity hospital,' the nurse, Valerie Dutton, protested.

'We've got no choice,' Cameron said. 'There isn't

time to wait for an airlift. The head's on show. Now get me what I asked for—now!'

'Don't push yet, Kelly.' He turned back to his patient. 'Just breathe quick and shallow—pant—don't push until we're ready.'

'I can't help it…' Kelly cried out in distress. 'Oh, God! Help me…the pain is too much…'

Valerie Dutton returned with the IV trolley, then left for more gear.

'Holly, can you get an IV line in for me and start saline?' Cameron asked.

'Of course I can.' Holly rummaged through the drawer and chose a large bore canula and tourniquet and after a minute's effort the canula was in.

Cameron quickly drew up ten milligrams of diazepam and administered the drug IV. He settled Kelly back and encouraged Tony to support her by holding her hand and helping to remain calm. Valerie returned with piles of sterile linen, another trolley and an instrument pack. Holly helped open the gear and set out the instruments, pouring sterile warm saline into one of the bowls.

'We're nearly there, Kelly,' he said as he scrubbed at the sink. He exchanged a quick glance with Holly as he donned a sterile gown and gloves.

Holly gave him a worried look in return.

'It's coming!' Kelly gasped.

Cameron reached between the young woman's spread legs and, taking the baby's head, gave the head and shoulders a gentle rotation as he instructed her to push. 'That's it, Kelly. Push now.'

Holly felt a lump come into her throat as the wizened and reddened baby emerged, the tiny mewing cry as he took his first breath of independent life pulling on her heartstrings.

'You've got a beautiful baby boy!' Cameron informed the parents, a huge smile taking over his face and brightening his eyes to a brilliant green.

Holly watched as Kelly and her husband embraced, the tears of relief and joy flowing freely.

'Holly, open the artery forceps and scissors on to the trolley; I need to cut the cord.'

Cameron took a clamp and clamped and cut the cord and, once the nurse had cleaned the tiny face, placed the tiny wriggling body on the new mother's chest.

'How about that, eh? Well done, Kelly. What a little champion he is.'

'Thank you… Oh, thank you…' Kelly choked with overwhelming emotion as she tenderly cradled her newborn son.

'We'll weigh him and clean him up a bit and then you can have him back for a decent cuddle,' Cameron said as he took the baby from her and handed him to the nurse. 'Have you got a name for him?'

Kelly smiled up at her husband. 'We thought we'd call him Jacob, didn't we, darling?'

Tony gave a proud grin. 'Yes, it's my second name.'

'Congratulations to both of you,' Cameron said as he worked to deliver the placenta and checked for abnormal uterine bleeding. Thankfully, there was none. He gave a deep inward sign of relief. Unlike the last tragic time, this had been a normal textbook delivery.

Holly did her best to keep up with Cameron's long strides as he left the ward a short time later.

'We've got an afternoon clinic in a few minutes,' he said as he glanced down at his watch. 'But I've got to check on a patient in the nursing home.' He turned to the right and threw over his shoulder, 'Tell Karen I might be a few minutes late.'

'Dr McCarrick?'

Cameron turned to look at her. 'Cameron,' he corrected.

'Cameron.' She moistened her mouth but for some reason the slightly tingling sensation of his name on her lips remained. 'I—I wanted to apologise for losing my temper earlier. I'm not usually so…'

'Stuck-up?' he offered.

She frowned at him. 'You think I'm stuck-up?'

'I think you should loosen up a bit. Patients pick up on stress signals. You were like a coiled spring in there. The Springtons had their own stress—they didn't need yours to deal with as well.'

Holly's eyes flared with anger. '*I* was stressed? What about you? You were the one with the clenched jaw and rigid spine when that car pulled up!'

'Which I had under perfect control by the time the patient was under my care. That young couple have been to hell and back and I didn't want them to think for a moment they were in any danger of having history repeat itself. We're the ones supposedly with the training and skill to deal with an emergency with unflappable clinical calm.'

'You don't think I have what it takes, do you?' she accused. 'Right from the moment I drove into this godforsaken place, you decided I wasn't suitable.'

'From what I can tell so far, your attitude is what is unsuitable; as for your skills—that remains to be seen. And this is not some godforsaken place, as you so charmingly describe it. It's the home of some fifteen thousand people who need us at any hour of the day to treat them.' He shoved the door open with his shoulder. 'I've got work to do. I'll see you later.'

Holly stared at the doors left swinging in his

wake, wishing she could think of something caustic to fling at him, but for once her quick tongue refused to co-operate.

She gnawed her bottom lip for a moment. Had she been so transparent? Certainly Baronga Beach wasn't exactly her idea of a career-advancing position but she'd comforted herself that at least for the next twelve months she wouldn't have to run the risk of bumping into her ex-fiancé with the gorgeous Sienna Salisbury on his arm, proudly flaunting her priceless wedding and engagement ring ensemble.

But had she made a mistake in running away without truly considering what she was getting into? She hated to admit it but Cameron McCarrick was very probably right. This wasn't the big city with reliable back-up within easy reach if her confidence was ever put to the test. This was a small coastal country town with limited resources. The small community was dependent on the only doctors in town. And she could no longer rely on other people to take charge if things got rough. She was on her own... Well, maybe not quite all alone... Cameron McCarrick was to be her partner for the next twelve months.

She gave a wry grimace as she pushed open the door to the consulting rooms. That was if she didn't throttle him first.

* * *

Holly had just finished treating a ten-year-old boy with an ear infection when Karen gestured to her as she approached the reception desk for the next patient file.

'Can I have a quick word with you, Holly?' she said in an undertone.

'Sure.' Holly followed Karen out to the small filing nook at the back of the reception desk.

'I thought I should warn you about who your next patient is,' Karen said.

Holly looked down at the patient file she'd just picked up, her eyes widening a fraction when she read the name of the convicted murderer Karen had told her had recently resettled in the district. The date of birth showed the patient was now in his early forties, and there was a black marker tick in the box next to 'Aboriginal and Torres Strait Islander'.

She did her best to disguise her reaction when she looked back at the receptionist. 'It's all right, Karen. As far as I'm concerned he's a patient just like any other.'

Karen's eyes narrowed and she leaned closer so her voice wouldn't carry through to the waiting room. 'He killed a sixteen-year-old girl. He took her life and yet he still gets to have one. It's not fair. They should have locked him up and thrown away the key.'

Holly compressed her lips for a moment. This was probably not the time to tell Karen about her cousin's conviction. Although she'd always been a firm believer in the punishment adequately fitting the crime, she had lost faith in the prison system through seeing what had happened to Aaron.

'Look, I've dealt with all types of people before. I'm sure I'll be able to handle it.'

'I suggested Mr Maynard see Cameron but he flatly refused. He wanted to see you. Be careful, Holly. You're not dealing with a normal person.'

Holly did her best to dampen down her own doubts as well as the receptionist's. 'Stop worrying, Karen. He's served his time and has some sort of rights, surely? Maybe he's really sorry for what he's done. You have to give people a second chance. We all make mistakes at times and some people make ones that have very costly outcomes which they regret for the rest of their lives.'

'Yeah, well, maybe you should talk to Tina Shoreham's parents about second chances and forgiveness before you go defending that creep. Trust me, Holly. This town can do without him coming back here. I just know there's going to be trouble.' Karen stalked back to the desk at reception and plonked herself down in the chair and reached for the telephone which had just started to ring.

Holly sighed and went back to the waiting room and called for Mr Maynard, trying her best to ignore the filthy looks he received when the two other patients waiting heard his name being called.

'Hello, I'm Dr Holly Saxby,' she introduced herself once he had sat in the chair by her desk in her consulting room. 'What can I do for you, Mr Maynard? I gather you asked to see me specifically.'

Noel Maynard sat on the edge of the chair, his chocolate-brown eyes darting about the room before briefly meeting hers. His hands were tense where they clenched the arms of the chair. Holly couldn't help noticing the nervous jiggling of his right leg until he got control of it by planting his foot a little more firmly on the floor.

'I need a prescription for some tablets,' he said. 'I ran out about two months ago and I'm not supposed to stop them.'

'What medication are you on?'

Noel fumbled in his top pocket and produced a small empty bottle and handed it to her. Holly looked at the label, which was clearly marked with the icon of Her Majesty's Prison Service and underneath: *Penicillamine 250g—take one tablet four times daily, two hours before meals.*

'These pills, Mr Maynard, are they for arthritis?

They seem an unusual treatment these days for that. Do you have rheumatoid disease?'

'I don't like being called Mr Maynard,' he said, his eyes falling away from hers to look at his fidgeting hands in his lap. 'And no…I don't have arthritis. It's in my records there; I've got copper disease.'

'Copper disease?' Holly frowned.

'Yeah…Wilson's disease,' he said, dragging his eyes back up to hers. 'I was diagnosed when I was a teenager. I've been on the drug ever since.'

'The penicillamine, you mean? That's why you're taking it?'

He gave a small nod. 'The doctor who was here when I was a kid diagnosed me. Dr Cooper was his name.'

Holly listened with one ear as she did a rapid search through the undergraduate lecture material she'd crammed somewhere in her head. She wasn't completely certain, but as far as she could remember the incidence of Wilson's disease in an indigenous person was extremely rare, if not unheard of.

'You're of Aboriginal descent, Noel, and you say you've been on penicillamine for how many years now?' she asked as she glanced down at his file in front of her.

'Aboriginal, yes. My family has lived on this coast for generations way back. I was diagnosed with copper disease at eighteen, so…twenty-six years.' His dark features twisted as he continued, 'I suppose you know I've been inside for twenty-five. I just finished my sentence a couple of months back.'

'Yes, I'd heard…' Holly wasn't sure what else to say.

'I wasn't going to come back here,' he went on, his eyes moving away from hers once more. 'I know I'm not welcome around here. But my mother is elderly, and…well…I wanted to spend some time with her before she…' He cleared his throat and added in an almost inaudible tone, 'Before it's too late.'

'I understand,' Holly said. 'How are you settling in?'

He gave a shrug of one thin hunched shoulder, his expression marked with deep regret and sadness. 'I didn't expect it to be easy. I know this sounds weird, but I kind of got, you know, sort of used to institutional life.'

'I've heard it's really tough in there,' Holly said, thinking of the harrowing distress on her cousin's face the last time she'd visited him. It had haunted her for days afterwards. It *still* haunted her.

He gave another tiny shrug. 'Yeah, it is, but you learn to play by the rules. I didn't have any choice. I didn't want to let the system beat me.' He paused for a moment before adding, 'Maybe in a way it helped me.'

'Helped you? In what way?'

His dark eyes met hers shyly. 'I wasn't much good at school… I got suspended a few times, then expelled. Mum didn't have the money to pay for the bus to send me to Jandawarra or some place else. So I just bummed around, trying to do odd jobs.' He looked away again. 'When I went to prison I couldn't read and write. I'd always thought I was dumb. But then the education officer helped me. Now I can read and write. I finished my high school education.'

'That's wonderful, Noel. What an achievement.'

His mouth moved upwards in what could almost be described as a smile. 'I went on and did some other certificates and stuff…computers and that sort of thing. Mum…she's proud I didn't turn out like my father.'

'Is your father still alive?'

He shook his head. 'No, he died just before I turned sixteen. He couldn't handle the drink… He'd go crazy on it—' he gave a small grimace '—more than crazy, once. Down at Jandawarra, he got into a fight at the pub and stabbed a bloke. Wasn't seriously injured, but one of his friends came after my father and stabbed him to death behind the rubbish bins.'

'That's terrible…' she said. 'That must have been so difficult for you at such a young age.'

He released a small sigh. 'I reckon if he hadn't got

stabbed that night he would have come home and laid into my mum big time. He did that a lot. I tried to stop him a few times but…' He let the sentence hang, as if recalling the memory was too painful.

In spite of his criminal background Holly couldn't help feeling sorry for him. She'd seen studies about abuse and violence in childhood which had clearly shown that such an environment was a breeding ground for future criminal behaviour. It took a special person to rise above it and choose another pathway from that modelled by their parents or primary caregivers.

Noel Maynard had had everything against him from the start. He was a full-blood Aboriginal who had grown up during a time when racism was rife in the community, especially one as small and parochial as Baronga Beach. He'd had a drunk and violent father and, after his father's brutal death, a disrupted education. He'd been a prison statistic waiting to happen, and it had happened—tragically. And not just for him but for the girl he had murdered and her still-grieving and angry family and friends, not to mention his own elderly mother, who must have suffered terribly in such a closed-minded town such as this.

'I don't want to take up too much of your time,' he said, shifting nervously in his seat. 'I'm in pretty good health apart from the copper thing. I'll just get my script and get back to Mum.'

'Sure, Noel. Yes, a script.' Holly reached for her prescription pad and began filling it in. 'But I'd like you to come back and see me in a few days. I'd like to go through your notes to familiarise myself with your case and I'd also like to run a couple of blood tests on you to—'

'No blood tests.'

She looked up at him in surprise at the sudden vehemence in his tone. His eyes were wide with fear and he'd pushed himself out of his chair as if uncertain whether she was going to jab him right then and there.

'You don't like needles?' She hazarded a guess, having seen a similar reaction too many times to count in her short time as a GP.

He gave a visible shudder. 'I don't have anything to do with needles. Ever.'

Holly wondered how best to deal with this, tapping her fingers on the desk beside the pathology form she'd reached for.

'Listen, Noel. You should at the least have your sugar and cholesterol done. If it's any reassurance to you, I'm known to have a good strike rate at getting the vein first go and—' She stopped mid-sentence when he sprang out of his seat and thumped the desk with his hand, his dark eyes spitting chips of rage at her.

'I told you—*no* needles.'

Holly swallowed as she leaned as far as she could back in her own seat, her stomach churning in fear. The sudden wildness in his dark eyes was frightening, as if he would do anything to stop her from taking blood from him and not regret it for a moment.

'It's all right…' She pushed the pad away with a shaking hand. 'No blood tests.' She took a calming breath but it did little to dispel her fear. 'Please sit down…Noel. It's all right, I won't take blood.'

'Sorry…' he mumbled as he resumed his seat, his anger disappearing as if it had never been. 'It happens every time…I can't control my reaction. I just can't stand the thought of a needle in my arm.'

Holly looked at him thoughtfully for a moment. Aaron had told her IV drug use was rife in prison, especially amongst long-serving inmates, and yet here was a convicted murderer who clearly had no stomach for it. She wondered what he'd seen while serving his sentence—perhaps he'd seen the damage drugs could do and so had avoided them.

'You really do have a full-blown phobia about needles, don't you?'

He gave her a quick glance and stared back at his

hands. 'Not just needles. I just don't like the sight of blood, my own or anyone else's.'

Holly wanted to ask him if he'd felt the same revulsion when he'd strangled and stabbed Tina Shoreham, but she decided it wasn't safe to do so. On the surface he appeared to be a nervous and shy man in his early forties, but she'd seen the flash of rage that had lit his eyes from behind when he thought she was going to insist on taking blood.

You are sitting less than three feet away from a man who killed a sixteen-year-old girl, a voice in her head reminded her. *He could reach out right here and now and squeeze the life out of your throat before you could even call out for help.*

Holly forced herself to remain calm and professional but still her stomach fluttered with unease and her heart seemed to be trying to make its way out of the wall of her chest every time Noel Maynard so much as shifted a millimetre in his chair.

'Th-there are programmes you can do,' she said into the silence that had fallen heavily. 'Desensitisation programmes that allow sufferers of all sorts of phobias to get on with their lives without the reaction you're having now. Would you like me to organise something for you?'

He shook his head. 'No… I don't have a driver's

licence yet so I can't drive to any appointments. And anyway, I have to look after Mum.'

'How did you get here?' she asked, knowing the only bus in town was the school bus and, as it was the summer holiday, even that wasn't running at present.

'I rode my mother's bicycle to town,' he said. 'It's not too flash but it gets me around.'

'Does your mother have a car?'

'No. But I'm going to get some work and buy one so I can take her places.'

Holly wasn't sure that he was going to have too much success finding employment judging by Karen's reaction to the news he was back in town. If the receptionist's reaction was any indication of the rest of the town's feeling, Noel Maynard was in for a hard time ahead, even if a small part of her felt he deserved it for what he'd done all those years ago.

'I'd still like you to come back and see me next week,' Holly said. 'Or perhaps you'd prefer to see Dr McCarrick instead?'

The flash of anger made a brief reappearance in his dark eyes when they met hers. 'If I don't get an appointment with you I won't be seeing anyone else.'

'Have you met Dr McCarrick?' she asked.

He shook his head. 'I don't have anything to do with male doctors any more.'

'I see…' Holly wondered what had happened to make him so adamant about seeing her and only her. She knew all about cavity searches from what Aaron had briefly told her. She also knew that not all prison doctors acted with the same professional code that people on the outside expected.

'Since you don't want to have a blood test, how about a urine test instead?' she suggested. 'We can do quite a few health-type checks on urine.'

Noel appeared to think about it for a moment. 'All right. I guess I can do that.'

She handed him a urine specimen container and directed him to the men's bathroom, advising him to leave the container with the receptionist on his way out of the clinic.

He gave a silent nod of agreement and, clutching the container, gave her one last unreadable look and left the consulting room.

Holly let out a sigh of relief as the door closed on his exit. Apprehension had crawled all over her skin the whole time he'd been sitting there, observing her with those dark eyes. Dark eyes that twenty-five years ago had watched a girl take her last breath while his hands had been around her slender throat.

She suppressed a little shiver and, swinging her seat around to face her desk, her eyes fell to the brown file of notes in front of her. The pages were yellowed with age, dry and crackling, as she turned through them page by page. The doctor's handwriting was almost impossible to read in places but she could see that Noel had been brought in by his father as a small child with a burst eardrum, for which Dr Cooper had prescribed antibiotic drops. The writing became more difficult to read on the next few pages and, because she was aware there were still patients in the waiting room, she closed the file and put it to one side to read more thoroughly later.

Just then the intercom on her desk buzzed and Karen's voice came through urgently. 'Holly, we have an emergency coming in. Cameron's still tied up in the nursing home. You'd better come out and get started until he gets back.'

CHAPTER FIVE

HOLLY rushed out to reception to find a man had just arrived with his left arm wrapped in a dirty piece of fabric, blood dripping all over the floor.

'I've cut my arm with a chain-saw,' he gasped, swaying on his feet.

She led him through to the emergency room next door, doing her best to calm him as she asked him his name.

'Jack Gordon,' he responded. 'Where's Dr McCarrick?'

'It's all right; I'll soon have you sorted out. How did it happen, Mr Gordon?'

'I was trimming a fence post...and the saw bounced off the barbed wire on to my arm...' His face drained even further of colour.

She helped him on to the procedure bed as Valerie Dutton appeared. 'I need a firm bandage to control this bleeding,' Holly said.

'Where's Dr McCarrick?' Valerie asked.

'This needs attending to now,' Holly insisted. 'I can't wait around for Dr McCarrick to show up. Pass me a crêpe bandage and get me a large bore canula and warm normal saline, stat. Get Karen to organise an ambulance for immediate transfer to Jandawarra for definitive treatment. Is there another nurse to help me stabilise the patient?'

'I'll call for Jenny Drew.'

Holly reinforced the ragged wound dressing with a crêpe bandage over the top. She was more than a little relieved that she could remember her EMST primary survey, even if she hadn't confidently demonstrated it in her practical exam a few months before—A, B, C–C–circulation with haemorrhage control.

She inserted a large bore canula into the undamaged arm and started running in a litre of warm normal saline full bore, doing her best to keep calm and in control, at least on the outside.

She'd done a term in A&E but she'd never been personally responsible for managing a major injury before—she'd always just observed as more senior doctors took control. Now, for the first time, with no warning and no support, she was in the firing line, directly responsible for the care of a significantly injured patient. The amount of blood Jack Gordon had lost was worrying—he looked pale, was becoming slightly confused and was cold and clammy.

She administered five milligrams of IV morphine, two grams of penicillin IV and took blood for cross-match, addressing Valerie as she returned from organizing the ambulance call. 'Get Jenny Drew to check the fridge for O negative blood. And Valerie, get me a suture tray stat, and gown and gloves.'

Holly applied a tourniquet to the man's left arm above the bandages while Valerie set up the instruments. She uncovered the wound to find a deep ragged laceration through the front of the elbow, clearly severing the brachial artery, the accompanying veins and possibly the median nerve.

'We have to transfer you to Jandawarra, Mr Gordon,' she addressed the ashen-faced patient. 'You've severed the main artery to your arm and it needs to be repaired within about an hour, otherwise you could lose the arm. I'm going to re-bandage the laceration to control the bleeding again, cool the arm with ice packs and release the tourniquet periodically to let in any blood from collateral circulation briefly without letting you bleed out.'

'Just sew the thing up!' Mr Gordon slurred roughly. 'I've got another fence to finish before nightfall.'

Holly gave him an incredulous look. 'You can't possibly do any such thing, Mr Gordon. If we don't get this seen to as soon as possible you'll be fencing for the rest of your life with a stump instead of a limb.'

He gave her glassy-eyed look and growled, 'Where's Cameron McCarrick? I want his opinion. You look too young to be a doctor, anyway. Nurse! Get me the proper doctor. *Nurse!*'

'Listen, Mr Gordon.' Holly injected her tone with steel. 'You have lost a lot of blood and are in no fit state to—'

'Well, if it isn't Jack Gordon causing trouble again,' drawled Cameron as he sauntered in. 'What have you done this time? Cut off your arm?'

'He's got a deep laceration to his—' Holly began.

'He looks like he's in shock. Have you called for blood?' Cameron asked as he inspected the wound.

She ground her teeth and bit out, 'Yes.'

'How far away is the ambulance?' he asked the nurse.

'Could be over an hour getting here, then two hours to town.'

'Call for patient airlift instead,' he said, donning gloves and goggles and reapplying the tourniquet. 'I want him in Sydney, not Jandawarra. This needs microsurgery. You'd better call and warn them at the receiving hospital. St George is closest with that facility.'

Jenny Drew returned with two units of O negative blood.

'Holly, attach one of those to your IV, run it in stat, then the other. And, by the way, didn't they teach you in your EMST course to wear eye protection when dealing with trauma? Jack here could be Hep C positive for all you know. An eye splash could finish your career right here and now,' Cameron pointed out as he finished firmly bandaging the arm and removed the tourniquet. 'Jenny, check the obs, please.'

'Pulse one hundred, BP 120/70, Dr McCarrick.'

'Good, he needs continued IV resuscitation but he seems stable at the moment. Pain OK, Jack?'

'What pain, Doc? Do I have to go to Sydney? You're here now. You can fix it.'

'Sydney for sure, Jack. Sorry. Your arm needs to be put back together again—you need a full-blown surgeon and operating theatre. You won't be chain-sawing for a couple of months.'

Holly waited until the airlift team had taken Jack Gordon away before she turned to face Cameron. 'I'd like a word with you.'

'I'm already late for my clinic,' he said.

'What I have to say won't take more than a minute or two.'

'Save it, Holly. I have a full list of patients who've already been waiting well over an hour.'

'I didn't think it was appropriate of you to take over my handling of Mr Gordon. You made me look as if I didn't know what I was doing.'

'Did you know what you were doing?' he asked.

She stiffened. 'Of course I did! I controlled the bleeding, administered fluids and pain relief and or-ganised for immediate transfer.'

'To the wrong hospital. Jandawarra is almost two hours away, far too late to have saved that arm even if there had been someone qualified there to perform microsurgery, which there isn't.'

'How was I to know that?'

'You should have asked.'

Holly bit her lip. 'All right...so there's no doubt I need to learn some local knowledge, but my basic medical skills are good and I don't think it's fair to criticise those, especially in front of patients and staff and especially when it's not warranted.'

Cameron scraped a hand through his hair as he looked down at her. Maybe she was right. He was being a bit hard on her. She'd only started that morning and it was undoubtedly a big change coming here from a city hospital. But her imperious manner had got under his skin from the start, reminding him a little too much of his ex-fiancée, Lenore. Holly's flashy red sports car and designer clothes all spoke of an attitude to life he had no time for.

But she had agreed to work here, which he knew from experience was more than a lot of newly quali-fied doctors would do. He could tell it wasn't exactly her first preference but he would have to make the best of it until someone else came along.

'Look, let's just get on with the day's work and in future if you're not sure about anything just ask me, right?' he said.

'Fine.' She gave him a resentful scowl as she made to brush past. 'That's if I can find you.'

'I told you I had to see a patient in the nursing home. I thought it was going to be a quick check-up but I ended up having to speak to the relatives about palliative care. Karen could have put you through to the extension or you could have called me on my mobile. I have it on me at all times. Hasn't she given the number to you?'

'I think she must have forgotten to. By the time she showed me around this morning the patients had already started arriving.'

'Here.' He handed her a card with his name, email address and contact numbers on it.

Holly took the card from him, her fingers brushing

against his. She looked down at the card rather than meet his eyes, wondering why her stomach was doing a fluttery sort of dance all of a sudden.

'Holly.'

She slowly raised her eyes to his. 'Y-yes?'

His blue-green eyes seemed to hold hers for an interminable pause before he finally spoke. 'Karen told me Noel Maynard had booked in to see you today. I take it she filled you in on his history?'

'Yes…' She unconsciously began to fidget with the card in her fingers. 'I saw him just before Jack Gordon came in.' Just as well, she thought wryly as she recalled the amount of blood the farmer had trailed in his wake. If what Noel had said was true about his aversion to blood, he might have totally freaked out, which would have terrified the patients in the waiting room, not to mention Karen.

Cameron's gaze slipped to the nervous actions of her fingers before returning to her eyes. 'Did you have any trouble with him?'

She decided against telling him of the one incident when Noel had seemed so threatening. 'No…he was…' She hunted for a word or phrase to describe her impression of the patient. 'He was…not quite what I was expecting.'

One of his brows lifted slightly. 'Meaning?'

When she didn't answer immediately he asked, 'Have you ever treated an indigenous patient before?'

Holly couldn't help feeling a little annoyed by the tone of his question. Was he assuming that her North Shore upbringing and training had made her totally ignorant, or even racist?

'Yes, as a matter of fact I have,' she answered. 'I spent three months in Alice Springs on an infectious diseases rotation.'

He didn't seem either impressed or surprised by her answer, which for some reason made her feel even more annoyed. That three months had been one of the most difficult and heart-wrenching terms she'd ever experienced but she'd come through it feeling as if she had grown as a result. She felt she now understood some of the issues that indigenous people faced and had grown far more tolerant as a result.

'Noel Maynard has spent a very long time in prison and has only been back in town a short time,' Cameron said. 'If you have any concerns about him at any time please don't hesitate to discuss them with me. Rob Aldridge, the local cop, will be keeping a very close eye on him. But if at any time you feel uncomfortable about being his doctor then I will happily take over.'

'Karen said he wanted to see me and only me.'

'I know. But we're talking here about a man who killed a young girl when he was just nineteen years old. He might be totally rehabilitated and I certainly hope and pray he is, but you are a single young woman, new to the district, and I wouldn't want you to be exposed to unnecessary risks until we know for sure if he is going to re-enter society appropriately. For all you know his supposed aversion to male doctors could be a complete ruse. He might have only insisted on seeing you because you are female and vulnerable.'

'If he doesn't see me he won't see anyone else,' she said. 'He told me that himself.'

'So you agreed to be manipulated just like that? Come on, Holly, next you'll be telling me you believe he's completely innocent.'

Although she'd had no real intention of defending Noel Maynard, something about Cameron's censorious tone incited her to shoot back, 'Not everyone who goes to prison is guilty. The legal system is far from perfect.'

'Evidence is evidence and if you want to see it first hand, why not ask Rob Aldridge to access the photos taken of Tina Shoreham after her murder? I haven't seen them personally, but her mother is my patient and what Noel Maynard did to that young girl was brutal. Lisa has had at least three nervous break-downs and Grant Shoreham hasn't worked in years; his life ended the day his daughter was murdered. Before you go championing Maynard's cause around town you should consider the Shorehams' feelings. They now have to live with the possibility of running into their only child's killer on a daily basis.'

Holly opened her mouth to respond but he'd already turned away, his long strides eating up the corridor, until she was left staring at the doors down the end swinging shut as he disappeared through them.

CHAPTER SIX

HOLLY sat on the back porch of the cottage later that day and breathed in the salty sea breeze coming in from the bay. The sun was still hot and high in the sky and the thought of a quick refreshing dip in the cool blue water was suddenly irresistible.

Her first day had been exhausting and she dreaded to think what the rest of the year would be like if things continued in the same way.

The beach was only a few blocks away so she slipped on her yellow and white daisy-topped sandals and a pair of denim shorts and a cotton T-shirt over her bikini and headed towards the shore.

A small group of young surfers were lying on their boards way beyond the breakers like a pod of dolphins waiting for the next wave. At the far end of the beach Holly could just make out the solitary figure of a girl walking a small dog.

Holly left her towel and outer gear on the sand and

walked tentatively into the sea, sucking in her breath at the first lap of cool water around her thighs. She wasn't a super-confident swimmer in the surf but she knew if she kept close to shore the chance of being dumped by a wave would be less likely.

She splashed around in the white foamy wash, ducking under the water up to her shoulders to cool off but not feeling game enough to go right under. She was glad no one was watching; she'd been meaning to take some stroke improvement classes for ages but ever since she'd qualified as a doctor there just hadn't been time. Her ex-fiancé, Julian, of course, was a fabulous swimmer and had even trained with the Olympic squad until he'd pulled out to pursue his career in plastic surgery. She'd gone to the local swimming centre with him a few times but he hadn't been particularly patient as a teacher and she'd headed to the kiddies pool and waterslide instead so he could get on with his lengthy training swims.

She turned her back on the ocean for a moment to look at a figure who had just wandered down the rocky path to the beach. The tall frame of Cameron McCarrick was easily recognisable even though he'd exchanged his casually neat working clothes for his faded board shorts and reflective sunglasses, a beach towel slung over one broad shoulder.

Holly turned around just in time to see a bigger than normal wave heading towards her. She tried to avoid its impact but in her haste her feet tripped over a small sand bar. She stumbled for a moment and almost managed to get upright again when the wave hit her in the back, sending her sprawling head first into the swirling sand of the bottom. She struggled to her feet, eyes and nose streaming, her sinuses shrinking painfully at the influx of briny water forced through them.

She opened her stinging eyes and turned just in time to see the next wave coming at her, but before she could get her feet into gear it too knocked her down, this time filling her mouth with water.

She coughed and choked but couldn't inflate her lungs properly. Oh, God! she thought. How can I possibly be so stupid as to drown in ten inches of water?

Suddenly a pair of very strong arms hauled her upright and carried her out of the surf. She blinked open her eyes at the same time Cameron let her body slide down the full length of his as he placed her gently on her feet on the dry sand.

'Are you all right?' he asked, frowning down at her in concern.

She couldn't speak—her throat was so raw from the salt—but her stomach did a funny little skip when she realised just how very close his hard male body was to hers. There was almost no space between them. She could even feel the rough masculine hairs of his thighs against hers as he steadied her against him.

'You must have aspirated some water,' he said. 'It's happened to me once or twice. Just take your time and try and breathe normally. You'll feel better in a moment.'

She did as he said but it was difficult to concentrate with him holding her so closely. She could feel…*no, you can't*, she corrected herself swiftly…you're imagining it. He's not getting aroused just because he's holding you! He doesn't even *like* you. He thinks you're incompetent and you've just given him more proof by practically drowning in water shallower than a baby's bath.

Cameron edged himself away from Holly's slim frame. His reaction to her surprised him. She was off-limits as far as he was concerned. She was a city chick who had 'temporary country term' written all over her, but no man with a pulse wouldn't allow himself a second look at her in a bikini.

He permitted himself another quick glance.

Her breasts certainly hadn't looked quite that generous in her work clothes, the two tiny triangles of hot pink Lycra showing them off to maximum effect. He forced his gaze away from their perfection to her toned stomach and then on to her long and smooth legs with just the right amount of healthy colour.

Yep, definitely worth a second look.

He suppressed an inward grin, however, when he brought his gaze back to her face. She had panda eyes where her mascara had run and her nose was bright pink with a sprinkling of tiny freckles over the small bridge that she very clearly despised if the amount of foundation she normally wore was any indication.

'Feeling better?' he asked once she'd stopped coughing and spluttering.

She nodded her head and wiped at her eyes, grimacing when she saw the black smudge on the back of her hand.

'I must look a complete mess,' she grumbled. 'God, I can't believe I got dumped like that.'

'It's not a pleasant experience,' he agreed, perversely thinking of Lenore, the first time he had in months. 'Why don't you sit down for a while and get your breath back? I'm going in for a quick swim. I'll walk back to town with you.'

Holly watched as he sprinted off to the water, his tall, tanned and lean body slicing through the rough wash so easily she couldn't help another cringe of embarrassment at her pathetic attempt at swimming.

She stared at her crimson-painted toenails for a

moment or two, determined not to watch him carve through the water like an iron-man, which would only make her feel all the more ridiculous, but as if they had a mind of their own, her eyes gradually crept up to follow his movement through the surf.

He was certainly a strong swimmer, she decided. He dived under each incoming wave on his way out and struck out beyond the breakers to swim in a straight line with strong, smooth and even strokes, turning his head alternate sides to breathe. His tanned skin glistened in the afternoon sunlight, his well-developed muscles leaving her in no doubt of his superb physical fitness.

She gnawed her bottom lip for a moment. What was she thinking, looking at him like that? He was a jerk. A practical joke-playing jerk who thought she was a city blow-in with no practical skills.

A tiny voice inside her head niggled that perhaps his assessment of her was right, but she just as quickly squashed it. Yes, her confidence had taken a bit of a hammering with Julian's defection, but her time at the Mosman clinic had been a rewarding one.

But too secure to really test you, that same little voice niggled at her again. You had expert advice and equipment at your fingertips. You didn't have to question your judgement for a second. Someone was always there to take over if things ever got out of hand.

She got to her feet in agitation. She had to stop this negative thinking. Before she knew it she'd be a cot case over every sore throat that came in, imagining it to be meningococcal disease.

Her gaze shifted to the other end of the beach. The small dog she'd seen with the girl was sprinting towards her, his little red lead bouncing along behind him, but the girl who'd been with him before was nowhere in sight.

The dog came up to her, panting and yapping, his little brown eyes looking up at her as if to work out if he knew her or not.

'Hey, what's wrong, little guy?' Holly bent down and gave him a scratch under his rough, hairy chin. 'Where's your friend?'

The little dog whined and looked back the way he'd come.

Holly usually had no time for people with anthropomorphic notions where their pets were concerned, but somehow this time she felt sure the little mutt was trying to tell her something.

She peered into the distance, wishing, not for the first time, that her long vision was better. She could make out the far end of the beach where a rocky outcrop was situated but it was still a blur.

Cameron suddenly appeared by her side, his body

still dripping water. He stooped to give the dog a quick scratch. 'Hey there, Scraps, what are you doing here all by yourself? Where's Belinda?'

'The girl he was with earlier was walking down that end of the beach but he's come back without her,' Holly said. 'I think he's trying to tell me something.'

Cameron flipped his wet hair out of his eyes, his mouth tilting slightly. 'What exactly did he say?'

She gave him a withering look, knowing she sounded like an idiot, but gut feeling was gut feeling, after all. 'He looks upset. I think he's worried. He came from down the end, running at full bore.'

Cameron's gaze shifted from hers to inspect the far end of the beach, his eyes narrowing in concentration.

'Can you see anything?' she asked.

'I'm not sure, but just to be on the safe side we'd better head down there to check. It's not likc Bclinda to let Scraps loose like that.' He thrust his feet back into his worn trainers and started sprinting down the beach, tossing over his shoulder that she should follow him.

Holly looked down at her bikini top. Running in two rather small triangles of fabric was just asking for trouble. This was definitely a decorative-only bikini, not one suitable for a jog along a beach that was looking longer every second as Cameron ate up the sand with his long, strong legs.

She tossed on her T-shirt and shorts and followed him down the beach at the most comfortable pace she could manage. As she got closer she could see Cameron scrambling up and over the rocky outcrop to get to what looked like a body at the base of a six-foot cliff.

'Hurry, Holly!' he called out as she approached. 'She's fallen and the tide's coming in.'

Holly tried to stop herself panicking but she just couldn't help it. The girl hadn't looked much older than fifteen or so. How would her parents feel if she had fallen and injured herself seriously? She'd seen depressed skull fractures and c-spine injuries before and lives permanently changed as a result, not to mention the non-survivors. What if Belinda was one of them, her life cut short before she'd had a chance to experience anything?

Stop it! she remonstrated with herself. Don't be so negative. The girl's probably just slipped and sprained her ankle. A pressure bandage and a bit of sympathy will fix her.

She scrambled over the rocks to where Cameron was assessing Belinda's condition, slipping and grazing one of her thighs on the rocks as she momentarily lost her footing. She bit back her cry of pain and struggled on until she landed beside him.

'She's fallen about six feet.' Cameron filled her in as he checked Belinda's pupils. 'Her pupils are equal, thank God. She was lying on her side, unconscious, with grazes to her face and shoulders.'

Belinda stirred and groaned slightly as Cameron gently brushed back her hair from her face.

'Belinda? Can you hear me? What happened?' he asked.

There was no verbal response.

'She's not responding to voice but airway and breathing are OK. GCS looks about eight or nine. We need to get help quickly, Holly.' He glanced up at her. 'Do you have your mobile with you?'

She shook her head.

He muttered a curse that she didn't quite catch. 'Run back to town and organise an ambulance out here stat, and tell them we're ultimately going to want another helicopter transfer to Sydney. Tell them we've got a head injury. There's no way we can deal with that down here.'

Holly's thigh was starting to really sting by now and her legs felt like sandbags as it was. 'Can't I stay here with her while you go back?' she suggested hopefully.

Cameron frowned at her. 'In case you hadn't noticed, the tide is coming in, and rapidly at that. I hardly think your level of confidence in the water is going to be particularly helpful for Belinda. Besides, she's a solidly built girl; you'd never be able to lift her.'

'But I—'

'Do as I say!' he commanded as a spray of water came over the rocks. 'And give me your T-shirt. I need it for a neck brace.'

Holly stared at him. *Her T-shirt?*

Cameron rolled his eyes. 'If it's not too much bother,' he added tautly.

Holly ripped it over her head and only just managed to stop herself flinging it at him in anger. She turned on her heel and scrambled back over the rocks, this time giving her knee a decent knock on a sharp edge on the way down the other side. She did her best to ignore the pain and was about halfway up the beach when she heard a whimpering sound and looked down to see the dog was running alongside her, his little pink tongue hanging out.

'You look as exhausted as I feel,' she panted and she scooped him up in her arms and half ran, half hobbled, as fast as she could the rest of the way to the clinic.

Once Holly had organised an ambulance she grabbed a sterile gown and covered her near-naked body to wait for the ambulance to pick her up as arranged.

'I've organised for someone to collect the dog,' Nicola Jessup, the nurse on duty, said.

'Thanks,' Holly said gratefully. 'The poor little chap was exhausted.'

'I must say, for a new doctor in town you've had one hell of a start to your year with us.'

'Tell me about it.' Holly grimaced as she caught a glimpse of her face and hair in the reflection of the glass. 'Is it usually so dramatic around here?'

Nicola shook her head, her tone dry. 'God, this place is normally so quiet even the church mice have left town for more action. You've just struck one of those days. Every country outpost gets them occasionally. Trust me, in a few weeks you'll be crying out for something to do other than seeing coughs and colds.'

'Has anyone rung Belinda's mother?' one of the other nurses on duty asked on her way past.

'Good thinking,' Nicola said and reached for the phone. 'You want to do it, Holly?'

The ambulance siren sounded in the distance and Holly shook her head. 'No, I've got to go down with the ambos to show them where Belinda is. Try not to worry the mother too much. It might not be too serious and it would be a shame to upset her unnecessarily.'

'Ambulance is here!' someone called out and Holly raced off, wondering how Cameron was coping with Belinda and the rising tide, and if the words of reassurance she'd asked to be relayed to the girl's mother weren't going to come back and haunt her…

CHAPTER SEVEN

CAMERON looked up in alarm at the rising surf. It was starting to crash over the rocks and spray over them both.

He'd rolled Holly's T-shirt into a loop and fashioned a soft cervical collar and carefully placed it around Belinda's neck to protect as best as possible from neck movements. If he had to move her because of the encroaching waves he knew it could compromise her neck stability. If she had a significant cervical injury he could turn it into a neurological one and cause paraplegia or quadriplegia. Belinda had not long ago moved her limbs so there didn't appear to be a gross spinal cord trauma.

He maintained her in the lateral position, the posture into which she had fallen, supporting her jaw to maintain her airway. He gave the surf another worried look, but over the sound of the crashing waves he heard the sound of the ambulance roaring down the beach. He let out a sigh of relief. 'Not long now, Belinda. Hold on there; we'll get you out of here and safe in no time.'

Holly watched as Cameron supervised the ambulance team as they shifted Belinda on to the spine board, applying a hard collar and oxygen. The young girl was then transferred into the back of the ambulance where he inserted an IV and reassessed the primary survey.

The helicopter hadn't yet arrived when the ambulance drove slowly and smoothly off the beach and up to the clinic.

'You'd better go out and speak to Belinda's mother while I keep an eye on things here till the airlift arrives,' Cameron suggested to Holly. 'Sandra could do with a bit of female support right now.'

Belinda's mother was distraught at the thought of her daughter having to be airlifted out of town for neurological assessment in Sydney. Holly did her best to comfort her while they waited for patient transfer but wasn't sure if anything she said was really helping.

'Your daughter will get the best of care in a large city hospital, Mrs Proctor. Try not to imagine the worst... Belinda is young and healthy and will hopefully spring back in no time at all.'

Sandra Proctor's face crumpled anew. 'She's all I have… I'm a single mother…there's just Bindi and me…and Scraps…' She choked on another sob. 'She really loves that dog. She found him as a stray…he's everything to her…'

Holly patted her on the arm reassuringly. 'Don't worry about Scraps. Nicola Jessup has organised one of Belinda's friends to take care of him until you both get back from Sydney.'

Sandra looked at Holly, her eyes red-rimmed. 'W-what if Belinda doesn't come b-back? Or what if she doesn't come back the same…you know…b-brain damaged or something?'

Holly swallowed the lump of dread in her throat. She'd spent a term at a rehabilitation centre and had seen first-hand the devastation of a life permanently changed after brain injury. Short-term memory loss, change in personality, loss of abilities that before the injury were taken for granted, such as being able to eat and drink without assistance or use the bathroom unaided. She'd seen young people forced to live like the very elderly, the loss of independence devastating for both the patient and their loved ones who were left to do what they could to care for them.

'Is there anyone I can contact for you?' she offered.

'A family member or friend who could support you right now?'

Sandra shook her head. 'There's no one... Bindi's father is...well, he hasn't seen her since she was about two so I hardly think he'd care now. I don't even know where he is or how to contact him.'

'The airlift team is five minutes away,' Cameron informed them when he came out of the emergency room. 'Belinda is stable, Sandra. She's still unconscious but we'll know more when they do a CT scan in Sydney.'

A short time later Belinda and her mother were on their way to Sydney in the helicopter after Cameron had briefed the care-flight doctor on board. Holly felt her energy drain away like the sound of the helicopter fading into the distance. Her thigh and knee were throbbing, her head was aching and she was thirsty and tired.

'Sorry about your T-shirt,' Cameron said just as she turned to leave. He handed it to her, soggy and wet.

'It doesn't matter; it wasn't an expensive one.'

He gave her a look she couldn't quite make out but she assumed he was mocking her as usual.

'What?' She gave him a little glare. 'You don't think I wear anything but designer-wear or something?'

Cameron's eyes flicked over her shapeless surgical

gown where small damp triangular patches from her bikini top were clearly visible. He hated admitting it but she looked absolutely gorgeous with her sand-encrusted hair, her freckles on show and her smudgy eyes looking too big for her heart-shaped face. She looked sweet and vulnerable instead of uptight and aloof, especially with her bare feet and crimson-painted toes peeking out from the trouser legs of the too-long scrubs.

'Where are your shoes?' he asked.

Holly bit her lip for a second. 'Down on the beach. I couldn't run in them so I left them behind. They're probably halfway to New Zealand by now.'

He gave a chuckle of laughter and her stomach did one of its funny little skips again at the deep rich sound. *OK, so you definitely have to get home and into a hot shower and away from this man right now*, she instructed herself sternly.

'I'll take a walk down there with you to look for them, if you like,' he offered. 'It's still light enough to see if they're still there.'

'It's OK, I didn't really like them all that much anyway,' she said, thinking of her throbbing thigh and knee.

'I suppose you have plenty more where they came from?'

Holly pursed her lips at the tone of his voice. What *was* it with his attitude?

'For your information, Dr McCarrick, I have a rather nasty scratch on my thigh and a bump on my knee so the thought of walking back down to the beach right now is not the least bit tempting, even—' she gave him a condescending look down the length of her nose '—strange as it may seem and no doubt crushing to your ego—with you.' With that brilliant exit line she began to flounce off but, to her annoyance, it turned into an ungainly limp. She didn't get far before a strong warm hand came down on her arm and turned her around.

'Are you hurt?'

For some strange reason Holly felt as if she was going to burst into floods of feminine tears. She positively *loathed* feminine tears but somehow her eyes were smarting and her chin wobbling and she felt the almost irresistible urge to put her head on his broad chest and howl.

'I...I slipped on the rocks...'

'Let me have a look,' Cameron said.

'I'll be fine—it's just a scratch.' She tried to brush him off but he was still holding her by the arm. She felt the warm slide of his hand moving down to circle her wrist and her stomach did another unexpected tumble turn.

'Come into the treatment room so I can have a proper look. It should be properly cleaned and covered even if it's not deep. I've seen some nasty infections from cuts and scratches from shells and shoreline rocks.'

Holly found herself being led along the corridor to a vacant treatment room. Cameron closed the door and instructed her to take off her scrub trousers.

'Um…' She hesitated. 'Could you turn your back?'

He gave her an ironic look. 'I just saw you an hour ago in the skimpiest bikini this town has ever seen. But if you insist.' He turned around, but not before she saw the movement of his eyes heavenward as if in search of patience.

Holly stepped out of the scrubs. 'OK. I'm ready.'

Cameron turned back around and looked at the long length of her legs, his eyes widening as he saw the ragged scratch on her thigh and her swollen knee.

'You should have told me you injured yourself.'

'I did.'

'I mean before,' he said, reaching for some betadine to cleanse the wound on her thigh.

'When before? *Ouch!*' She winced at the sting of the antiseptic on her raw flesh. 'I was organising an ambulance and airlift as well as trying to comfort Mrs Proctor at your direction, plus organise accommodation for Belinda's dog. I didn't have time to even think.'

'It's certainly been a busy day,' Cameron agreed as he pressed a sterile dressing on her thigh, doing his best not to notice how smooth and shapely her leg was. Clinical distance, he reminded himself. Think of her as a patient. But it was practically impossible with her so close. Her skin felt like velvet and, in spite of her dip in the ocean, the fragrance of jasmine clung to her lovingly. He found himself taking his time as he dressed her wounds, wondering what it would be like to have those slim legs wrapped around him.

Holly looked down at his dark head practically between her thighs as he began to inspect her knee. When was the last time a man had been that close…? She jerked back from her thoughts with a convulsive little swallow. What was she thinking? That Cameron McCarrick was a potential lover?

She sneaked a glance at his face, his expression full of concentration as he moved from dressing her thigh to examining her knee.

'Does this hurt?' Cameron palpated the swollen joint.
'No…*aahh!*'

He stressed the knee sideways, then, with the knee at ninety degrees, rocked the joint back and forth.

'Ligaments are intact, but you've certainly stressed the joint. I'm putting on a firm crêpe bandage to reduce swelling and I want you to use crutches for a few days and not bend the knee.'

'*Crutches?*' She gaped at him. 'That's overdoing it, isn't it? I'll look ridiculous hobbling around like an invalid tomorrow on my third day in town.'

'That's what I recommend, Holly. I did enough time as a football team doctor in Melbourne to know a potentially significant knee injury when I see one, and how to minimise the risk of exacerbating it. Now, do you want me to bandage it properly or are you going to treat it yourself?' He met her eyes challengingly.

'Oh, all right, bandage it.' She gave in grudgingly. 'As long as I don't have to rub in liniment and smell like a footballer.'

Cameron firmly bandaged the swollen knee with a couple of six-inch crêpe bandages, fixing them firmly with tape.

'We'd better measure you for armpit height,' he said, handing her a pair of crutches.

Holly looked down at her swinging legs as she tested them. She met his amused eyes as she handed them back and her heart did a little skip when his fingers touched hers as he took them off her.

'What about these?' He handed her another pair.

She gave them a try and managed a decent distance without too much trouble.

'I think they'll do,' she said. 'But are you sure this is really necessary?'

Once again his eyes met hers and her breath seemed to stop somewhere in the middle of her chest.

'Keep your weight off it for a couple of days and it will be fine,' he said and added with a little wink, 'Trust me, I'm a doctor.'

She gave a groan and hobbled to the door.

'If you give me five minutes I'll jog home and bring my car back to take you home,' he said.

Holly wanted to resist the offer but she was beyond the reach of her pride. 'Oh, would you really?' she said, instantly wishing she hadn't sounded quite so pathetically grateful. A simple thank you would have done but the touch of his hands on her bare legs had unsettled her more than she'd realised.

He held the door open for her. 'Hop into the waiting room and I'll be back in two minutes.'

A short time later Holly eased herself into the car with Cameron's help. He pulled out the seatbelt and she felt the slight brush of his arm across her chest as he handed it to her to fasten, her pulse rate skyrocketing at the feel of the hard male muscles against her softness.

'I'm just going to do a quick detour to the beach to see if your sandals are still there,' he said as he got in the driver's side.

She decided against protesting that they were probably long gone. 'OK. Thanks, I'd appreciate it.'

She sat in the car while he went down the path to the beach, her eyes following him as he hunted along the fringe of sand. After a while he came back up the path empty-handed and gave her a rueful look as he got back behind the wheel. 'My guess is Auckland.'

She fought against it but in spite of her efforts a reluctant smile stretched her mouth. 'Do you ever take anything in life seriously?'

He backed the car out of the space before answering. 'Sometimes, but life is short and if you don't make the most of it, it will pass you by while you're complaining about what's wrong instead of what's right.'

She angled her gaze his way. 'So what brought about this optimistic philosophy of yours?'

He met her eyes briefly before turning back to the turn-off to their street, his expression giving little away. 'I guess you could say I spent some time in the school of hard knocks. I have since learned to take each day as it comes and live it to the full.'

Holly thought about his answer as a silence slipped between them. Erma Shaw had told her about the break up of his relationship with his fiancée and how deeply it had affected him. Holly wouldn't have picked him as a particularly heartbroken man but she wondered if his laugh-at-life attitude was a smokescreen for deeper pain that he didn't want to have on show.

When it came down to it she knew her experience with men was a bit limited. She was an only child of two very affluent parents who'd spent the very few years they'd been married fighting volubly and the many years since their divorce silently feuding, using her as a sort of go-between. She wasn't particularly close to her father, who at times was bombastic and a little too forceful in his opinions, most of which were in direct contrast to hers. He still considered her a fool for studying medicine instead of law, as he had done with spectacular results, which even now he couldn't resist reminding her of repeatedly. As one of Sydney's leading barristers, it was impossible to win an argument with him and she had more or less stopped trying years ago.

Her only cousin Aaron hadn't lived close by, so the times she'd seen him during her youth had been too few and far between for her to get to know him very well.

She'd had one or two boyfriends, none of them really serious until Julian Drayberry, who had promised her so much but in the end given so little. It suddenly occurred to her that Cameron McCarrick was unlike any man she'd ever met before. She chanced another covert glance at him as he pulled into his driveway.

He was certainly handsome but it was almost as if he was totally unaware of it. Unlike Julian, she recalled somewhat wryly, who had spent more time in the bathroom doing his cleansing and moisturising routine than her, refusing to go out in public without his thirty-plus sun protection on.

Cameron, on the other hand, moved with a freedom in his body as if he was totally at home in it no matter how it was dressed or groomed. He was equally comfortable in worn and faded board shorts with his tanned chest bare, or dressed in neat casual clothes while he dealt with patients at the clinic. She hadn't seen him in a suit and tie, but imagined he would look rather impressive with his tall, lean build and compelling eyes. He was confident without being over the top like her father, and competent and caring with patients. He could handle gruff old farmers like Jack Gordon with a relaxed joking manner and yet care for an injured teenage girl with obviously tender concern.

'Is your knee hurting?' Cameron asked, rocking her out of her reverie as he came around and opened her door for her.

'No...yes...I mean a bit...' She hobbled out of the car with his support, her cheeks suddenly feeling hot as his warm fingers cupped her elbow.

'I've got some Panadeine Forte in my doctor's bag. I'll get you settled inside and give you some.'

Holly felt a fool for needing so much help on her first full day in town and couldn't quite rid herself of the impression that he thought she was proving to be even more incompetent by becoming injured during the rescue of a patient. Here it was, Day Two, and she was on crutches. How on earth was she going to get through a whole year?

CHAPTER EIGHT

CAMERON came back with the tablets a few moments later, to where Holly was leaning against the kitchen bench, her second glass of water in one hand, her crutches put to one side to give her already aching armpits a rest.

'You might get a bit drowsy with the codeine, but it should wear off by morning,' he said as he handed the pills to her.

'Wow, your opinion of the new training scheme for GPs must really be at rock-bottom if you think you need to tell me the side effects of a simple drug like Panadeine Forte,' she said before she could stop herself. 'I do have my very own copy of MIMS, you know.'

He folded his arms and gave her a musing look for a long moment. 'You really are very well named, aren't you?'

'What do you mean?' She stiffened.

'Holly is a rather pretty shrub with bright red

berries and very sharp thorns.' His mouth tilted sardonically. 'Yes, I think your parents named you very well indeed.'

Her eyes flared in instant anger. 'Oh? And no doubt your name means a smart jackass jerk with a perverse sense of humour!'

'No, it's Gaelic and actually means crooked nose.'

'Well, I'm very surprised you haven't been given one by now,' she quipped back. 'And let me warn you if you don't leave right this minute I might very well be tempted to give you one myself.'

'You want to hit me?' His tone was almost taunting, his eyes glinting with something she hadn't seen in them before.

No, right now I'd like to kiss you, a tiny voice said inside her head, but she very quickly stomped on it—hard. What on earth was wrong with her? He was laughing at her behind those green-blue eyes and here she was, fighting an attraction for him she just didn't understand.

'No...no, of course not, I was just—'

Suddenly he was standing way too close. Way too close to escape. Way too close to even breathe. She looked up into those sea-green eyes and swallowed as she pressed herself even further back against the sink until her spine protested at the pressure. The atmosphere was so heavy she could even hear the faint dripping of the kitchen tap behind her.

'W-what are you d-doing?' she stammered.

His chest was almost but not quite touching hers. She had only to breathe out fully and her breasts would brush his hard body. She felt as if she was going to drown in the unfathomable depths of his eyes as he leaned in even closer. She could smell the clean ocean saltiness of his skin and hair as well as the faint musk of a male who had been hard at it physically and hadn't yet showered. It was heady and intoxicating and made her suddenly ache to experience first-hand what his mouth would taste and feel like against hers. Her eyelids fluttered closed and her mouth opened just a fraction in anticipation of his kiss when she felt his arm brush past her waist to reach for the tap behind her. Her eyes sprang open at the sound of the tap being tightened.

'I was turning off the tap,' he said, stepping back from her. 'What did you think I was doing?'

'I…I…' She floundered for a moment. *The tap? He was turning off the dripping tap?* She could feel her face flaming. Oh, God! She'd been almost begging him to kiss her.

'This is a hot summer,' he said. 'It might not rain for months and the town water supply will be seriously compromised if you don't make sure every tap is turned off properly. And that means no long showers, either. If there's a bush fire in the district we won't be able to handle it if everyone in town uses water indiscriminately.'

'Is there anything else you need to tell me to make me feel even more incompetent?' she bit back crossly. 'I mean, apart from me being too much of an idiot to turn a tap off properly without the sort of brute strength someone like you obviously takes for granted?'

'Did I call you incompetent?'

'Not in so many words, but you imply it all the time.'

'How?'

'Down on the beach you thought me incapable of managing Belinda. You said with my level of confidence in the water I was hardly likely to help her. I wouldn't have even hurt my knee if you hadn't insisted I run back to town for help. You should have gone for help since you're supposedly the super athlete around here.'

'By the time the ambulance got there the tide would have already been lapping at Belinda's feet. How do you think you would have handled that?' he asked, a tiny flicker of anger burning in his eyes as he stared her down.

'If you had gone instead of me the ambulance

would have been there a whole lot faster so that's a moot point,' she argued. 'I had to run in bare feet with an injured knee. You had trainers with you. It was wrong of you to send me. It compromised the patient's safety as well as mine.'

'That's a whole lot of rubbish and you damn well know it,' he threw back, his tone tight with tension. 'I acted entirely appropriately under the circumstances. I assessed the risks and made the decision I thought would produce the best outcome for the patient's safety.'

'While seriously compromising mine,' she said.

'You know what your problem is?' he said, his jaw now visibly taut.

She gave him a churlish look. 'No, but no doubt you are going to tell me in point-by-point detail.'

'Damn right I am,' he growled back. 'From what I've seen so far you are a city chick with a serious attitude problem. From the moment you drove into town you've looked down your snooty little nose at everyone and everything. You're impulsive and irresponsible. That little near-drowning stunt down at the beach is a case in point. Apart from a few surfers who were too far out to help, you were on an unpatrolled beach, which with your inability to swim even enough to save yourself was just asking for trouble.'

'I can *so* swim!' Holly defended herself, secretly hoping he would never ask to see the evidence of her true capabilities. She knew that paddling around the toddlers' pool hardly qualified her for the Commonwealth Games, but she hated the fact that he had found yet another fault in her.

'How far can you swim?' he asked.

'I...' she faltered for a nanosecond '...a fair distance.'

'What sort of distance are we talking about? Two metres or two kilometres?'

'What business is that of yours? It wasn't stipulated on the application form that I had to be able to swim the length of the Baronga Beach in order to qualify for the post.'

'No, but it would help me to know your true capabilities so if an emergency occurs I will know how to manage it. This is a seaside town with its fair share of boating accidents. We had a drowning only last year, and in a place as small as this it affects everybody.' He scraped a hand through his salty hair, his tone softening a fraction. 'Look, if you need a hand with learning to swim I can give you a few lessons. There's a small shallow lake behind the sand dunes a little further down the coast. We could go through the basics there and build your confidence.'

'I don't need your help,' she said, folding her arms across her chest. 'And I am not lacking in confidence.'

Holly could tell he didn't believe her, which made her all the more angry towards him. She could just imagine how he would conduct his lessons with her, laughing at her for being so hopeless as soon as he witnessed her floundering out of her depth. Maybe that was why he was offering in the first place, not because he was concerned for her safety, but just so that he could make even more of a fool of her.

'Fine,' he said. 'If you want to drown in a puddle of water, go right ahead. But I'm not so sure I'd want to give you the kiss of life. You might end up biting my tongue off.'

'If you so much as dare to put your mouth anywhere near mine—drowning or not—I will do more than bite your tongue off!' she threatened with a fiery glare.

The air started to crackle with some indefinable tension as soon as her spluttering tirade left her lips. Holly could feel it like an invisible energy suddenly pulsating between their bodies. She could feel the tension growing in his body, standing so close. She could even see it in his blue-green gaze as it clashed and warred with hers.

'What gave you the idea that I would want to kiss you?' he asked.

She blinked at him for a moment. *God*, she thought. *Do I look that bad without make-up?* Yes, her hair was a mess and her freckles were no doubt all on show, but surely she wasn't totally undesirable. Or was she?

She quickly rustled up some much-needed feminine reassurance. Make-up or no make-up, she knew she had a figure that turned heads. She should know; it had cost her a fortune in gym memberships to get and maintain it.

She tilted her chin. 'You're a man, aren't you?'

'I was the last time I looked.'

For some reason Holly couldn't stop her gaze dipping to where the evidence of his maleness was housed behind the thin fabric of his board shorts.

She forced her gaze upwards with an effort, but she knew that the tiny swallowing movement of her throat probably betrayed her.

'And I'm not gay, if that's what you're thinking,' he said, filling the little silence.

'I—I wasn't thinking…that…'

'What were you thinking?'

There was nothing she could do to drag her eyes away from the magnetism of his. She felt ensnared by his gaze, making her feel vulnerable and exposed, as if he was seeing right inside her to where the real and very low level of confidence she possessed was secretly hidden. She'd worked so hard all her life to come across as self-assured and confident in all situations, but it was all a ruse and somehow she sensed he knew it.

'What were you thinking, Holly?' he repeated.

'Um…nothing… I was thinking nothing.' She gave her hands a dismissive little flap and shifted her gaze. 'You have a perfect right to consider me unattractive and I understand completely and—'

'I don't recall saying you were unattractive.'

Her head came back up. 'But you said you…you know… wouldn't want to…to…'

'Kiss you?' Cameron asked, his eyes going to the soft bow of her mouth almost of their own volition.

She ran her tongue over her dry lips in a nervous gesture that somehow surprised him. He had her picked as a street-smart city girl who was well prac-tised in the art of seduction, but right now she looked like a teenager about to get her first proper kiss. Her cheeks were softly flushed and her melted-chocolate eyes seemed to be almost alight with sparks of ten-tative anticipation.

'Do you want me to kiss you, Holly?' he asked, the movement of air from his mouth as he spoke brushing across her face like a caress.

She gave an almost undetectable little swallow as he brought his head down a fraction closer. 'D-do you want to kiss me?' she asked, her voice barely more than a husky whisper.

Cameron fought with himself for a long moment. This was total madness. He wasn't in the market for an intimate relationship and certainly not with someone who was more than likely going to hightail it back to the city before the month was out, let alone the whole year. He'd been down this pathway before. It had taken months to get over Lenore's decision to choose the city over him and he didn't want to make the same mistake twice.

He wished he could just step back from Holly and leave it to his imagination to conjure up the taste and feel of her in his arms, but something about her up-tilted face, with its dusting of tiny freckles, threw his self-control completely off course. Before he could stop it, his head came down even further, his eyes closing in time with hers as his lips found the unbe-lievable softness of her mouth.

Holly sighed as his mouth brushed against hers in a gentle exploratory kiss. She had been kissed too many times to recall each and every one but, for all that, she was certain no one had ever kissed her quite the way Cameron McCarrick did. His lips moved against hers with a sensual slowness that was totally captivating, making her breathless for more. She opened her mouth at the first stroke of his tongue along the seam of her lips and a heady rush filled her at the feel of that firm, insistent, very male warmth penetrating her softness to delve into and possess every secret place.

She felt his hands go to her hips and pull her closer, the probe of his aroused body sending a wave of wanting right through her. She could feel the silk of need between her thighs, her response to him so unrestrained it almost frightened her. Julian had been a methodical lover and she had certainly experienced pleasure in his arms, but never throughout his textbook-perfect repertoire had she felt this overwhelming urgency of need so quickly and so unrestrainedly.

She pressed herself even closer, relishing the sensation as Cameron's warm hands moved from her hips to the underside of her ribcage, not quite touching her breasts but close enough to build the anticipation of him doing so to fever pitch. She could feel the tight points of her breasts aching for his touch and her stomach gave a little flip of delight when he deepened the kiss as if his self-control had just slipped a fraction.

His mouth ground against hers without restraint, his earlier gentleness replaced by a fiery burst of male need that she could feel pulsing against her lower body.

His tongue swept over hers and captured it in an erotic dance that left her sagging against him with need. Her hands went to his waist and then, with a brazenness she had not realised she possessed, she touched him through his thin board shorts, stroking her fingers along his engorged length.

He suddenly wrenched his mouth off hers and held her from him, his breathing uneven as his eyes met hers.

'I don't think this is such a good idea.'

'You have someone else?' The question was out before she could stop it.

It was a moment or two before he answered. 'No.'

'So…' Holly wished she could control the heat in her cheeks but, without the screen of foundation, what could a girl do? 'You've still got feelings for your ex?' she asked.

Again he paused for a fraction of time before he answered firmly, 'No.'

'I see…'

'I know this goes against the grain of what most men my age say they want, but I really want more out of life than one-night stands,' he said. 'I want to settle down and have kids, to bring them up to appreciate the true value and quality of life. I don't believe you can get that quality of life in the city. But I have yet to find a woman who thinks and feels the same.'

Holly was more than a little surprised by his revelation. He was what—thirty-two or -three? Most men, including her ex-fiancé before he landed his socialite bride, were out there bedding every woman they could while they could get away with it, while way down here on the southern New South Wales coast was a guy who wanted to have what she had longed for all her life but had been denied. Her sense of family had been more or less destroyed by her parents' acrimonious divorce, and yet in a deep part of her she still hoped that somewhere out there was a man who had the same core values as she: a longing for connection, for intimacy, for loving stability in which to feel secure and grow in self-confidence.

'I'm sorry, Holly, but if you want a quick tumble in the sack to pass the time you've picked the wrong guy,' he said as he scraped a hand through his hair.

Holly's anger came to her rescue. 'You think me so desperate that I would consent to sleeping with you?'

One of his brows lifted a fraction at her venomous tone but she was undaunted. 'For your ego's information, I am not here in search of a husband or, for that matter, even a lover. I don't even *like* you. You are everything I most detest in a man. You're scruffy and unpolished and you have the arrested development of a pre-adolescent.'

'Well, since we're into character assessments, allow me to make mine,' he returned, his eyes beginning to glitter at her warningly.

She folded her arms crossly and gave an exaggerated eye roll. 'Go ahead. I can hardly wait.'

'In my opinion you are totally unsuitable to this position,' he said. 'You're inexperienced and lack confidence. You are not what I was expecting when I asked for back-up. I have single-handedly run this clinic for months only to find the person they finally send me is a young woman who is more interested in whether her hair is in place than the welfare of her patients.'

'That is not true!' Holly said, unconsciously flicking a wayward strand of hair out of her face to glare at him. 'You have no right to say that. This is only my first day working here. How can you possibly assess my capabilities properly in such a short time?'

His gaze swept over her, lingering for a moment on her bandaged knee before returning to her face. 'Believe me, I've seen enough. You should put that knee up for a while. You won't be able to drive for a couple of days. I'll take you with me in the morning.'

'I don't need a lift. I can make my own arrangements.'

'Have it your way, but let me warn you it's a long hop to the clinic.'

Holly watched as he left the room, only releasing her tight breath once she heard the front door open and close again on his exit.

'I'll show you,' she muttered as she limped to where she'd left her crutches. She stuffed them under her arms and took three hops before tossing them to one side in disgust as she sat down in front of her laptop computer. 'If I have to crawl there on my belly, I'll show you, Cameron McCarrick.'

CHAPTER NINE

'GOSH, you're here early,' Karen said the following morning when Holly turned up at the clinic. 'I would've thought after all the drama yesterday you'd come in a little later. How is your knee?'

'Fine, I didn't need crutches after all, ' Holly answered, privately marvelling at the gossip hotline that had obviously been operating overnight, a night in which she'd spent several hours poring over her laptop and the Internet, re-educating herself in the details of Wilson's disease in between fuming over Cameron McCarrick, all the time trying not to think about *that* kiss.

'Have you heard how Belinda Proctor is doing?' she asked the receptionist.

'She's doing OK. There's a small fracture of the skull but they're not talking about surgery. She's not fully regained consciousness but they don't think there'll be any lasting damage.'

'That's good,' Holly said. 'I felt so sorry for her mother.'

'Yeah, she does it tough does poor Sandra.' Karen reached for some pathology reports on the desk. 'These came in first thing.'

'Thanks.' Holly leafed through them, frowning as she read the results.

'Can I get you a cup of tea? I'm just about to have one,' Karen offered.

'Thanks, that'd be nice.' Holly looked up from the pathology notes. 'But can you get me Mr Maynard's file first? I just want to check something.'

Karen went to the patient files, extracted the folder and handed it to her, the line of her mouth tight with disapproval. 'I hope he's not going to come to the clinic too often. It'll make things difficult for the other patients.'

Holly decided against reminding the receptionist that Noel Maynard had the same rights to medical attention as any other patient. It was a sensitive subject and clearly nothing she said was going to change it.

'What time is my first patient?' she asked instead.

Karen glanced at the appointment book. 'About forty minutes.'

'Good. I'll be in my consulting room if anyone

needs me before then,' Holly said, clutching the folder and doing her best to disguise her limp as she made her way down the hall.

Once at her desk she opened the patient file and began reading from the start, determined to make sense of Dr Cooper's notes in order to understand the pathology results Karen had just handed her. She'd been expecting elevated levels of copper to show up in Noel Maynard's urine specimen as he had been without penicillamine for two months, but the results had come back showing zero levels. That didn't make sense. In Wilson's disease the copper levels should have been elevated, even in a spot urine. The pathology report had recommended a repeat test with a twenty-four-hour urine sample. She examined the notes with concentration, reading past his childhood ailments to where Dr Cooper had documented the initial diagnosis of Wilson's disease.

The notes were hard to follow—not only was the writing difficult to read, but pathology reports had been sticky-taped on to sheets entitled 'MAYNARD, Noel' and the sticky tape had pulled off, leaving a jumble of loose pieces of paper with fading results. Two blood tests showed liver function tests, with grossly elevated serum transaminases. There was one blood test with a handwritten patient name in the top right-hand corner, 'Noel Maynard', showing an almost undetectable level of serum ceruloplasmin.

Holly's late-night revision had reminded her of the diagnostic testing for Wilson's disease, low ceruloplasmin being one of the important findings. The tests were certainly consistent with Wilson's disease but would hardly be considered definitive. She looked on further through the notes but there was no record of additional tests such as a twenty-four hour urine copper excretion, liver biopsy or a penicillamine challenge test.

She flicked back to the handwritten clinical notes. Wilson's disease was an autosomal recessive condition—the patient had to have inherited an abnormal gene from both parents. The parents could have been carriers or actually have had the disease. Effective treatment for Wilson's disease had only been developed in the mid-nineteen-fifties, but if either of Noel's parents had had the disease, would they have been recognised or treated way down here in the sticks back then?

She went all the way back through the early entries in Noel's notes, looking for any family history. There was none.

Karen came in with a small tray bearing a cup of

tea and a couple of plain biscuits. 'Here, this should get you going before the throng arrives,' she said.

'Thanks, Karen, that's nice of you. Listen, do we have a medical record for Noel Maynard's father? Do you know his first name?'

'Noel Maynard's father?' Karen raised her eyebrows. 'Warren Maynard? Why on earth do you want those? That whole family is nothing but trouble. Even the mother is a bit off the planet, though to be fair that's to be expected, married to that psycho and then having her only son turn out to be a murderer. Who wouldn't be a little crazy after that? She hides up in the hills like a hermit. Only the local pastor's wife and the delivery guy from the bottle shop are allowed on the place. She waves a rifle at everyone else. Her husband Warren was murdered in a pub brawl and I'm not the only one around here who thinks he had it coming to him.'

'I'd still like to see the notes if we have any,' Holly said, 'and his mother's, too, and any siblings'.'

'There was a sister but she left when Noel was arrested. Couldn't cope with the shame, I suppose. She was a nice enough kid but I reckon that background has triggered her to turn out the same. They often do. I reckon it's programmed into the genes.'

Holly was getting tired of Karen's undiluted

bigotry. 'The notes, Karen?' she reminded her again, her tone a little more demanding.

The receptionist pulled herself upright, her expression a little miffed. 'I'll have to dig them out of the archives. It could take some time.'

'Fine, as long as I can have them some time today. There are some family details I want to check on. The doctor's writing is almost impossible to read and I just want to make sure I haven't missed anything significant in the family history.'

'Dr Cooper's, you mean?' Karen asked.

'Yes. I suppose he's left the district by now?'

'Actually, he's a whole lot closer than you think,' Karen said.

'Oh?'

'Dr Neville Cooper is a permanent resident in the nursing home wing of the clinic,' Karen informed her. 'After his stroke about eighteen months ago he needed full-time care. His only son lives in Sydney so it was decided Dr Cooper would be better amongst friends down here. But it would be pointless trying to talk to him. If you think his handwriting from twenty-five years ago is hard to understand, try listening to him speak.' She gave a rueful grimace. 'It's so sad. His son visits him when he can but there's never any change. God knows why he's lasted as long as he has. He was the mainstay of this town for years—practically delivered my whole generation and even some of our kids. Now he's reduced to a dribbling figure in a chair. Life's cruel sometimes, isn't it?'

'Yes, indeed it is.'

The reception bell sounded and Karen reached for the door. 'That will be Mrs Spaulding with gout. Finish your tea and I'll send her in, shall I?'

'Sure.' Holly chewed one end of a biscuit and took a sip of tea once the receptionist had left the room. She looked down at the open file in front of her and frowned. She drummed her fingers absently on the desk, then, with a little sigh, closed the file and put it to one side.

Once the afternoon clinic was finished Holly made her way to the kitchenette where Cameron was already seated, one ankle crossed over his thigh in his customary casual pose, the newspaper spread out before him, a cup of coffee in one hand. She hadn't run into him so far that day. He'd been called out to a home visit over lunch and the rest of the afternoon had kept her occupied with a variety of routine consultations which had filled in the time rather than providing any sort of challenge.

'I see in spite of your doctor's orders you've apparently made a remarkable recovery,' he said as she came in.

Holly gave him a chilly look, sat down and reached for a chocolate biscuit even though she had no intention of eating it. 'You are not my doctor.'

'Maybe not, but I still think you shouldn't be using that leg to drive. Your car is a manual, right?'

'Yes.'

'You're taking a risk driving with a damaged knee. If you have to slam on the brakes in a hurry you could lose control of the car.'

'I am perfectly capable of driving. The crutches were total overkill. I'm not even limping.'

Cameron tossed the paper to one side and, uncrossing his leg, stood up and came around to where she was sitting.

'Lift up your skirt and show me.'

'I beg your pardon?'

'You heard me, Holly. Let me see how the swelling is.'

Holly tucked her legs under the table and smoothed her skirt even more firmly over her knees. 'I told you, I'm fine.'

He went back to his side of the table and picked up the newspaper again. '"Gemini",' he read out loud. '"Today you should take care not to be fooled by people who insist on pulling the wool over your eyes."' He lowered the paper and gave her one of his disarming grins. 'Pretty accurate, huh?'

She rolled her eyes and stuffed the chocolate biscuit in her mouth so she didn't have to answer.

'Listen to yours,' he went on as his gaze returned to the newspaper. '"There are uncertain stars around you at present. You need to check details very carefully in case you overlook something vitally important."'

'You're making that up,' she said, not quite able to control a little shiver that traversed the length of her spine.

He passed the paper over to her. 'Read it yourself. You're Sagittarian, aren't you?'

She took the paper but didn't look at it. 'How do you know I'm Sagittarian?'

'Your birth date was on your application form.'

'You surely don't take this stuff seriously, do you?' she asked.

'Not really, but I have a sister who's into all this stuff in a big way. A couple of days with her and I defy any sceptic to maintain integrity.' He reached across for one of the biscuits. 'According to Freya, your star sign is the luckiest of the zodiac.'

'Not so far,' Holly couldn't help inserting a touch cynically.

'Unlucky in love?' he said, taking a wild guess.

She met his eyes. 'I would appreciate it, Dr McCarrick, if you would not refer to my personal life.'

He threw back his head and laughed. 'Touché. Well done, Holly. I've been well and truly hoist with my own petard.' He took another chocolate biscuit off the plate, took a generous bite and, after he'd swallowed it, asked, 'So what was his name?'

'Whose name?'

'The guy who broke your heart.'

'No one *broke* my heart.'

'So for the heck of it you just put a pin on a map and randomly came up with Baronga Beach?'

'It wasn't quite like that…'

He surveyed her flustered features for a long moment. 'But you're running away, aren't you?'

She wanted to deny it but something about his softened tone and intent gaze found her confessing, 'It was eight weeks before my wedding. I had the dress made and the caterers booked.' She began to toy with a tiny crumb on the table. 'Julian decided we weren't suited after all.'

'There was someone else?'

'Isn't there always?'

She heard him release a sigh. 'Yeah, you could be right.'

Holly lifted her head to meet his eyes once more. 'What about you?'

'What about me?'

'I've told you my history. It's only fair you tell me yours. After all, if you don't, no doubt someone else around here will, with their own slightly embellished angle on it.'

'Yes, you could very well be right,' he conceded reluctantly. 'All right, here goes. I imagined myself to be in love with a woman I met at a Family Medicine conference in Melbourne about eighteen months ago. It was difficult conducting a long-distance relationship but I really thought we'd make it work. In the end she pulled the plug. She couldn't face a lifetime working in a country practice.'

'And you wouldn't compromise?'

He looked at her as if she'd just asked him to fly to Mars and back in a day. 'No,' he answered implacably.

'But why not?'

'It wasn't an option for me.'

'Why? Because you think a man's career is more important than a woman's?' Holly asked, a hint of feminist angst hardening her tone. 'That just because you're a man you get to choose where to work and live and whoever is unlucky enough to marry you has to trail along behind with no allowances made for her own career aspirations?'

Cameron's eyes turned a steely blue as he got to his feet. 'For your information, Holly, the reason I chose to live and work in an isolated area is because I grew up in the country and personally witnessed the tragic consequences of inadequately trained medical practitioners.' He gripped the back of the chair he'd just vacated and thrust it back under the table, rattling the cups and plates on its surface. 'I was thirteen years old when I watched my older brother bleed to death after a hit-and-run accident. If I had known then even a fraction of what I know now I could have saved him. And so could the attending doctor, who was almost as useless as I was. Don't tell me I'm the one who has to compromise. I promised Tyler I would do my best to never let something like that happen again and I swear to God no one, and I mean no one, will ever get me to change my mind or break my promise.'

Holly winced as he stormed out of the room, not quite slamming the door on his exit.

'What was all that about?' Karen came in a few seconds later carrying some patient files. 'Cameron looked like thunder just then. He practically bit my head off. I've never seen him lose his temper before; he's normally so easygoing. Did you say something to upset him?'

Holly took the files the receptionist had handed her. 'I think I might have touched a raw nerve. I won't do it again.'

Karen gave her a thoughtful look. 'You know, I've never really noticed it before, but you look a little bit like his ex-fiancée, Lenore Forsythe.'

'I do?' Holly unconsciously clutched the files closer to her chest. 'In what way?'

'Your shape and colouring are different but you have that just-stepped-out-of-a-fashion-magazine look,' she said. 'Did you do some sort of grooming course?'

'No…I just like make-up and nice clothes.'

'Well, you won't find too many fancy clothes down here,' Karen said, giving her own plain outfit a disparaging glance. 'The nearest boutique is in Jandawarra and it's hardly what anyone would call designer wear. But if you're looking for hard-wearing jeans and sturdy boots and industrial strength underwear then it's the place to shop.'

'Thanks for tracking down the files,' Holly said, changing the subject.

However, Karen wasn't so easily distracted. 'He was really in love with her, you know. He pretends he wasn't but we all know he's trying to put it behind him and move on.'

'What was she like?' Holly found herself asking after the tiniest pause.

'Lenore was outgoing and confident. Too confident, if you ask me, but then it takes all types, I guess. She works in Melbourne in a city practice. She's even treated celebrities, but of course she wouldn't say which ones due to patient confidentiality. She would have been an asset here with her connections but things didn't work out that way. She found Baronga Beach too quiet. She had a fling with someone for a while but, who knows, she might come to her senses. As far as we know she hasn't married anyone else yet.'

For some reason Holly felt a sinking feeling deep inside. She couldn't understand her reaction at all. It wasn't as if she was the least bit interested in Cameron McCarrick… Well, maybe a *little* bit interested, she reluctantly admitted. There was so much about him that she found annoying—but after his recent revelation she was beginning to realise his laugh-at-life attitude was a cover-up for deep emotional pain. He had lost his older brother in tragic circumstances. It had permanently changed him, had made him determined to do his bit to change the world.

It was impossible not to compare him with Julian Drayberry who, in spite of his natural talent for the mechanics of life-saving surgery, had switched specialities in order to pursue a lucrative career in plastic and cosmetic procedures instead. He'd even offered to enhance her figure for her, promising to schedule her in well before the wedding so she'd look perfect for the photos. She'd been knocked sideways by his offer, her self-confidence hitting an all-time low. She could see with the benefit of hindsight that their break-up had been inevitable, but at the time it had completely thrown her. Was it really too much to ask a man to love her just the way she was?

'You haven't got another patient until four-thirty,' Karen said, cutting across her private ruminations. 'I'll give you a buzz when they arrive.'

Holly gave her a weak smile and, taking the files back to her consulting room, sat at her desk and opened the first one.

It was marked: 'Warren Maynard—deceased'.

CHAPTER TEN

HOLLY read through the notes with difficulty, finding sketchy comments regarding poor general health, alcoholism, cirrhosis of the liver and one comment: 'examined in police cell—mentally unstable'. The last entry read: 'phoned by police/patient deceased/ stabbed in fight Jandawarra pub/bled out'. So, formal pathology testing had never been done on Warren Maynard. No actual diagnosis of Wilson's disease had been made.

She turned to the next folder—Betty Maynard's. Apart from the birth of two children, Noel's mother had visited the doctor rarely. There were a couple of notes regarding a sprained wrist and a black eye, and another a few months on documenting a cheek laceration needing stitches. Dr Cooper had scribbled a few notes here and there but there was no record of any general health testing being carried out, such as routine pap smears, mammograms or blood screens for thyroid function or haemoglobin. Betty Maynard hadn't even been to see Cameron.

Holly sat back in her chair and gave the end of her pen a nibble. If Betty Maynard was a carrier of Wilson's disease a blood test would prove it. Medical technology had progressed exponentially over the twenty-odd years since Dr Cooper's notes and Noel's diagnosis had been made. The genetics of Wilson's disease was now known. It could be possible to detect the genetic abnormality for the disease in Noel's blood. An abnormality in chromosome thirteen had been discovered in the nineteen-nineties, a gene which coded for a protein that transported copper from the liver into bile. In Wilson's disease this protein was defective—copper accumulated in the liver, causing cirrhosis, and eventually spilled back into the blood, allowing it to accumulate in the brain, causing tremors and mental instability, and into the kidneys and the cornea, causing kidney failure and a copper-coloured corneal ring called a Kaiser-Fleischer ring.

The chances of doing any genetic testing on Noel's father, a man who had been dead for over twenty years, were slim indeed, but Holly couldn't help hoping that she could somehow talk Noel into a blood test or a twenty-four hour urine sample at the very least. A liver biopsy would be more definitive, though from what she'd seen so far of him she didn't like her chances of getting that. However, a home visit so she could meet his mother certainly wouldn't go astray. She jotted down the address and placed it in her bag under the desk.

Tossing her pen to one side, she closed the files and locked them into her desk drawer just as Karen buzzed on the intercom about the arrival of her last patient for the day. Holly fixed a smile on her face and went out to the waiting room to greet the teenage girl who had served her in the General Store the first day she'd driven into town.

She glanced at the file she'd picked up from the reception desk to check the teenager's name. 'Hello, Jacinta. I'm Dr Holly Saxby; come through.'

She waited till the girl was seated in her consulting room before opening the file. 'Now, what can I do for you?'

The girl gave her a very direct look. 'I want to go on the pill.'

Holly flicked her eyes back to the date of birth on the file in front of her. According to the records, Jacinta had only just turned fifteen. She met the girl's somewhat defiant stare across the table. 'Have you discussed this with your parents?'

Jacinta gave her a brooding look. 'My real father is dead. I live with my mother and stepfather.'

'I see.' She waited for a couple of seconds before asking, 'Are you in a sexual relationship at present?'

Jacinta lowered her gaze a fraction without answering.

'You're only just fifteen. Surely you can afford to think about it a little longer before you take that very big step?' Holly suggested gently. 'The legal age of consent in this state is sixteen. If the person you are considering sleeping with is above that age he could be charged with carnal knowledge.'

'I want to go on the pill,' Jacinta insisted. 'I've got trouble with my periods and I've heard it can help.'

'What sort of trouble are you having?'

The girl lowered her eyes once more. 'They're not regular.'

'When was your last one?'

Jacinta shrugged one shoulder. 'I dunno…six weeks ago or something like that.'

Holly felt her stomach cave in slightly. This young girl had her whole life ahead of her. She was supposedly here for contraceptive advice but Holly's gut feeling was indicating that the horse from this particular stable might have already bolted.

'Have you had unprotected intercourse during that six or so weeks?' she asked.

The girl's expression grew petulant. 'I don't have to answer that.'

'No, you don't, but I'm afraid I can't write a prescription for the contraceptive pill to someone of your age without one of your parents' consent. I could organise an appointment for you and your mother so we can discuss some options. Would you like me to do that for you?'

The girl gave her a surly look from beneath her lashes. 'I thought you'd be different.'

Holly frowned. 'What do you mean?'

'Dr McCarrick is a man. I can't talk to him. I thought you'd be able to understand.'

'I do understand, Jacinta,' Holly said. 'More than you realise. I know teenagers think anyone over the age of twenty is practically ready for the grave but, like you, I've had to make the sort of decisions you're having to make. Taking a relationship to that level needs careful thought. There's so much more to a physical relationship than simple gratification of desire. No form of contraception is totally foolproof, apart from abstention. Condoms and the pill have a failure rate. That needs to be factored in, especially in someone of your age. Why not think about it a bit more and come back and see me with your mum? That way we can discuss the options more openly.'

Holly could see the girl wasn't happy but there was nothing she could do to change it. The law was the law. Everyone knew kids all over the planet flouted it but what else could she do? She was new in town. If word got around that she had prescribed the contraceptive pill for someone underage, what would the repercussions be? There was a chance the girl was already pregnant. A consultation with the parents in that case would be far more constructive than anything else.

'I'm sorry, Jacinta,' she said. 'I'd really like to help you but without your parents' consent my hands are tied.'

Jacinta got to her feet, her eyes still downcast and her expression sour. 'I'm sorry for wasting your time, then.'

'You haven't wasted my time. It was nice to meet you properly. How often do you work at the General Store?'

'A couple of afternoons a week.'

'Have you lived in Baronga Beach all your life?'

'No…just since my mother remarried.'

Something about the tone of the girl's voice suggested to Holly that things weren't all that happy at home. She'd heard the same quality in her own tone in years gone past, pretending things were fine when they weren't.

'How well do you get on with your stepfather?'

Holly could see that her question had startled the girl. Although she tried to hide it behind a coolly impersonal façade, Holly could see the tension in the girl's shoulders and the way her eyes flickered with something indefinable but no less disturbing.

'Jacinta?' She softened her tone even further. 'Would you like to talk about it?'

Jacinta shook her head and lowered her eyes once more, staring at her sandalled feet. 'There's no point. My mother is happy for the first time in ages. My dad was killed when I was twelve…'

'That must have been very difficult for you.'

The girl gave a shrug that on the surface seemed dismissive but Holly was well aware of the cover-ups teenagers used to disguise their pain.

She took out a card and wrote her mobile number on it and handed it to the girl. 'If you change your mind about that chat, give me a call. I grew up with a variety of stepfathers so I know a little about how hard it is to fit in a blended family.'

Jacinta took the card and stuffed it into the pocket of her jeans with a mumbled word of thanks.

Holly inwardly sighed as she accompanied the

young girl back out to reception. Sometimes it was very hard to maintain a professional distance. Every now and again a patient would slip under her defences and wreak havoc with her clinical training.

'You look pensive,' Karen observed once Jacinta had left the building. 'Don't tell me Miss Sulky Pants got under your skin. She does it to everyone. She's a right little madam, that one.'

Holly frowned. 'What do you mean?'

Karen gave her a streetwise look. 'My daughter Erin's in the same class. Jacinta's a bully, and when she's not being a bully she's a troublemaker. Her mother is beside herself over how to handle her. Renee is married to the town mayor, Clinton Jensen. How do you think he feels to have his stepdaughter running amok?'

'What's he like?'

'Who? Clinton Jensen?'

Holly nodded.

'Well, for one thing he's done an awful lot of good for this town over the years. He's been instrumental in rebuilding the community centre after it was burned down a couple years ago by vandals, and he's the first on hand if there's an emergency. He drives the State Emergency Service vehicle.'

'What's he like as a person?'

Karen's eyes narrowed suspiciously. 'What's with the character analysis? Has that girl been planting silly ideas in your head?'

'What sort of ideas do you mean?'

'Look, Holly. You're new in town. This is your second day at work. In a few months you'll have most of the population figured out. In the meantime, take it from someone who knows. That girl is a troublemaker and she'll stop at nothing to get attention. She's manipulative and vindictive. She resents the fact that she now has to share her mother. It's as simple as that. She idolised her father and no matter how hard Clinton tries to take his place, Jacinta won't allow him to.'

Holly could see it was pointless taking it any further. She put Jacinta's file away as Karen shut down the computer and locked the desk.

'Sally, the other receptionist, is working tomorrow and Thursday,' Karen said as she stood up to leave. 'How is your knee holding up, by the way?'

'It's a bit sore but I'll rest it this evening.'

'Good idea. See you Friday, then.' Karen slung her oversized bag across one shoulder. 'Tony will lock up if you want to stay on for a few minutes. I've diverted the phone to Cameron's. He thought it best for him to do the on-call roster until your knee settles down.'

Holly felt a wave of shame pass over her face at the way she had misjudged Cameron. He'd put his personal prejudices aside to consider her welfare. It was the least she could do to go to his house and apologise.

CHAPTER ELEVEN

HOLLY knocked at the house next door but there was no answer. She could hear the sound of a power tool being used at the back of the house so, making her way around the uneven pathway, she came to where Cameron was up on a ladder with a drill, boring into the roof above his head.

She feasted her eyes on his tanned, muscular body. His work shorts made his long, lean legs seem to go on and on. His chest was bare and even from this distance she could see the trickle of perspiration running between his broad shoulder blades and the bunched muscles in his arms as he controlled the drill.

As if he'd sensed her presence, he turned and switched off the drill in his hand. Holly's neck protested at the height advantage but she found it hard to look away from the blue-green of his eyes as they met and held hers.

'Is this a house call?' he asked.

She gave the dilapidated construction he was working on a sweeping glance and quipped, 'Is this a house?'

He laughed and descended the ladder. Holly's tummy was still doing its funny little quivering dance by the time he came to stand in front of her, his smile lightening his eyes to a sea-green.

'It will be when I've finished with it,' he said, brushing some plaster dust off his face.

'Why don't you employ a builder to do the work?' she asked. 'Wouldn't it be quicker?'

'I like the work. My dad's a builder so it kind of runs in the family.'

Holly captured her bottom lip with her teeth at the mention of his family. 'I wanted to apologise for being so...so insensitive today...'

'Don't give it another thought,' he said, unplugging the drill from the power socket. He straightened and faced her once more. 'I was wrong to bawl you out like that. I don't often lose my temper but, I'm afraid, when I do, I don't do it in half measures. My sister tells me it's my star sign but I put it down to too much work and not enough play. You know what they say about all work and no play making a man very dull.'

'You're not dull.' The words were out before she

could stop them. Her face instantly flamed and she carried on falteringly, 'I mean, not in that sense…'

'I'm very glad to hear it,' he said, his eyes twinkling with amusement at her obvious discomfiture. 'How's the knee?'

'The knee?' She blinked at him. 'Oh, *my* knee… It's fine…just fine…' She ran her tongue over her dry mouth, her heart starting to pick up its pace as his gaze moved over her face. She felt her stomach tilt when his eyes went to her mouth and lingered there for a moment.

A light sea breeze began to play around them. Holly could feel it pick up her hair and lifted a hand to brush it back, but before she could locate the wayward strand Cameron's hand had captured it and gently tucked it behind her ear. The brush of his fingers on the sensitive skin lifted each and every hair on her head in delicious anticipation. His fingers were slightly rough, reminding her of his essential maleness. Her mind raced with images of how it would feel to have those work-roughened hands cupping the weight of her breasts, or sliding down the length of her thighs. She felt the pulse of desire beating a tattoo between her legs at the closeness of his heated body. She could even smell the slightly musky scent of his skin where the hot late-afternoon summer sun and physical activity had completely overridden his aftershave. It wasn't the least unpleasant; instead she found it incredibly arousing.

'Have you changed your mind about me examining it?' Cameron asked.

It took Holly a moment to figure out that he was referring to her knee again. Caught off guard, she stumbled out, 'Oh…not unless you think it's necessary.'

'Come inside out of the hot sun.' He led the way indoors. 'I've just about finished the kitchen.' He opened the door into the kitchen and pulled out a chair for her.

She sat down and looked around with interest. The final painting hadn't been done but the appliances, cupboards and bench tops were in place. It was similar to her house next door but with subtle differences here and there.

Cameron squatted down in front of her and she peeled back her skirt. Holly was so acutely aware of her body that the slide of the silky fabric along her leg felt like a caress and she had to force herself not to react in any way when his hands touched her.

'Does this hurt?'

'No…'

'What about this?'

'Not really…'

He got to his feet and held out a hand to help her up. She slipped her fingers into the warmth of his but, instead of letting go when she was upright, her fingers curled into his.

His gaze locked with hers.

'So here we go again,' he said with a touch of wry humour.

'W-what do you mean?'

'I was about to kiss you again and the rational part of me tells me not to, but the other part…'

Holly gave a tiny swallow. 'What's the other part telling you to do?'

He tugged her towards him and she had her answer. His hardness against her softness, the swell of his body a heady reminder of the dangerous water she was drifting into.

It was so out of character for her to be feeling so overwhelmed by desire. She hardly knew how to account for it. Surely it wasn't possible to fall in love with someone in the matter of two days?

'M-maybe I should just leave now…' The words stalled in her throat as he brought her even closer.

'Do you want to leave right now?' His voice was low and deep.

She looked into his eyes, which were burning

with desire and another quiver ran through her from head to toe.

'We're both recovering from broken relationships,' she said. 'We're doing the whole rebound thing. We hardly know each other. It wouldn't be right to...you know...get involved...'

'There are degrees of involvement,' he pointed out.

His statement brought her back to earth with a solid bump of reality. She stepped out of his hold and folded her arms tightly across her chest. 'You told me yesterday that you had no interest in one-night stands.'

'You don't strike me as a one-night stand sort of girl.'

'I thought you said I was a stuck-up city chick who looked down her—and I quote—"snooty little nose" at everyone and everything in town.'

'I might have overdone it on the nose bit,' he conceded with a little smile.

'I don't actually care what you think of my nose or any other part of my anatomy,' she tossed back. 'For your information, I came here this evening to apologise, not to fall into bed with you.'

'Batteries in the mechanical boyfriend not run out yet?' He winked at her teasingly.

Holly felt her face flood with heat. 'You're a jerk, do you know that?'

'You have mentioned that once or twice before.'

'No wonder your ex-fiancée dumped you. You're nothing but a big kid in a man's body. You don't need a wife, you need a nanny.'

'And I know what you need. It's written all over you.'

She gave him one of her best scathing looks. 'And what, pray tell, is that?'

He moved so quickly she had no time to step away. His hands captured her upper arms and brought her right up against his body so that not even a breath of air could separate them.

She opened her mouth to protest at his rough handling but the small choked sound was lost in the descent of his mouth over hers. It was a bruising kiss but she found herself responding to it all the same. Hot flames of need passed between their mouths. Holly could feel each and every scorch of his tongue as it blazed with searing heat against hers. He thrust, he probed, he darted and he swept every recess of her mouth until she was almost mindless with raging need. She kissed him back, her tongue flicking his with increasing confidence, her small teeth nipping at his bottom lip. She felt her skin grazed by his day's growth and a hot spurt of liquid desire anointed her intimately.

He pressed her back against the nearest bench, his hands sweeping underneath her silky blouse to cup her breasts. She felt the movement of his thumbs over her peaking nipples through the lace of her bra, and then her stomach did a total free fall when he thrust the flimsy garment aside to touch her naked flesh. She arched her back in pleasure, his lower body grinding into hers with unrestrained passion.

Somewhere in the distant recesses of her brain Holly could hear a phone ringing.

Cameron suddenly stepped back from her, his eyes still glittering as he snatched up his mobile from the bench at the other side of the kitchen. He barked out a hello but his tone instantly gentled when he recognised the female voice on the other end.

'Hi, Mum… No, of course not… Breathless? Do I?… No, I wasn't doing anything special. How are you and Dad?'

Holly took it as her cue to leave. She straightened her clothing and, sending him one last fulminating look, turned and left, her affronted stalk-like exit somewhat spoilt by the recurrence of her limp.

Cameron suppressed a sigh as the door snapped shut behind her. 'No, Mum, that was just a little whirlwind slamming the door. So, when are you and Dad heading down for a visit?'

When Holly arrived at the clinic the next morning, Sally Oldfield, the other part-time receptionist, intro-

duced herself and informed her that her first appointment wasn't until ten a.m.

'You can make yourself a cup of tea and take it easy
if you like. Karen told me you'd had a pretty hectic
start to your time with us.'

'Yes, it certainly was a baptism of fire. But I
think I'll give the tea break a miss. I thought I
might go and introduce myself to Dr Cooper in the
nursing home.'

'Good idea,' Sally said. 'His son visits as much as
he can but it's a lonely life for the poor old man.'

Holly made her way through the covered
walkway which connected the nursing home to the
clinic and asked the nurse on duty if she could see
Dr Cooper.

'Of course you can,' Meg Talbot answered with a
friendly smile. 'He's quite alert today, for a change.
I'm afraid his stroke has affected his speech but if
you listen carefully you can sometimes make out
what he's saying. I'm sure he'll be pleased to have
a chat with a fellow doctor.'

Meg led her through to a private room overlook-
ing the bay, where an elderly man was sitting in a
wheelchair, dressed in summer-weight cotton
pyjamas and slippers.

'I've got a visitor for you, Dr Cooper,' Meg said

cheerily. 'This is Dr Holly Saxby; she's the new doctor in town who's come to help Cameron.' She turned to Holly and said in an undertone, 'I'll leave you to get acquainted.'

'Thank you.'

Holly waited until the nurse had left before she approached the elderly man. 'Hello, Dr Cooper. I've heard so much about you I thought it high time I came to see you. How are you?'

It was a stupid question, she thought almost as soon as she'd asked it. That Dr Cooper thought so too was more than obvious. He mumbled something inaudible but she didn't really need to hear it to understand the general gist of it.

'I'm sorry; that was a bit insensitive of me,' she apologised.

He waved his good hand in a gesture of dismissal and mumbled something that sounded like, 'Forget about it.'

'Do you mind if I sit with you for a while?' she asked.

He looked at her through rheumy eyes for a moment before pointing to the chair just behind her, which she took as a yes.

She straightened her skirt over her knees once she was seated and smiled at him. 'So...this is a nice place you have here.'

He grunted in agreement and, using his undamaged hand, wiped a trail of saliva from the corner of his mouth. Holly's heart positively ached for him. She couldn't imagine what it would be like to be in his position in forty-odd years' time. She knew about the tendency amongst doctors to take their health for granted. They spent so much time dealing with other people's illnesses that at times it was all too easy to feel somewhat immune oneself. It must have come as a dreadful shock to be so disabled in such a way when for so many years Dr Cooper had treated others just like him in his care.

'Would you like me to take you out into the garden for a bit of fresh air?' she offered. 'I don't have any patients for at least an hour.'

If he was surprised by her offer he didn't show it. He simply pointed to a thin dressing gown lying on the end of the bed and she picked it up and gently helped him into it.

'It's quite warm outside but the sea breeze can be fresh,' she said as she turned the chair for the door.

Holly spoke with the nurse on the way past who smiled in gratitude, directing her to the ramp exit.

As soon as they made their way outside Holly saw Dr Cooper lift his face to the warmth of the sun, his eyes closing as he let its healing rays seep into his frail figure. She turned at the sound of slightly out of time marching footsteps and came face to face with Major Dixon.

'I see you've got one of the casualties there,' he said imperiously. 'Take him to the surgical tent immediately for assessment.'

Holly was nothing if not a fast learner. She schooled her features into respectful obeisance and gave him a quick salute. 'Yes, Major. Right away, sir.'

'See that you do,' he growled and marched on, mumbling something about soldiers in skirts and what in God's name was the army coming to.

She looked down at Dr Cooper, who was smiling somewhat lopsidedly. 'It's cute how everyone goes along with Major Dixon's time warp,' she said.

'Mmm,' he murmured his agreement.

She wheeled the chair a bit further until they came to a seat near the rose garden, the heady fragrance brought out by the heat of the sun.

'Is this OK here?'

He gave a single nod and she saw his nostrils flare slightly as he drew in the scent of the roses. She let the breeze and the distant sound of seagulls and terns fill the peaceful silence for a while, working up the courage to ask him about his diagnosis on Noel

Maynard. She wasn't confident he'd be able to tell her much, even if by some miracle he remembered, but she thought it was as good as any place to start.

'Dr Cooper—' she turned to face him '—I was wondering if I could talk to you about a patient of mine.'

He wiped another trail of saliva from his mouth and nodded his compliance.

'This particular person was your patient a long time ago. You diagnosed him with Wilson's disease. Do you remember?'

Out of the corner of her eye Holly saw his frail hand, grasping the arm of the chair, tense until the knuckles went nearly white.

'It's a very rare condition and since the patient was of Aboriginal descent I was wondering if you could remember the details of how you came to that initial diagnosis?'

Dr Cooper mumbled but this time she understood exactly what he had communicated. Her interview with him was well and truly over.

He tried to turn the chair around with his one good hand, which almost toppled him out of it. Holly only just steadied it in time.

'I didn't mean to upset you, Dr Cooper,' she said, trying to make amends. 'But Noel Maynard is my patient now. I had some unusual test results come back and I thought it would be best to ask your advice on how to interpret them.'

The elderly doctor grew increasingly agitated and in spite of his stroke-damaged speech Holly could make out the words 'murderer' and 'animal' as a track of tears joined the constant trail of saliva down his face.

'I'm sorry…'

'What's going on?' Meg Talbot met her at the door as Holly started to wheel him up the ramp.

She gave the nurse a helpless look.

Meg turned to a passing nurse and instructed her to take Dr Cooper back to his room for a rest before turning back to Holly. 'What happened?'

'I asked him about a patient of mine he'd treated in the past.'

'Which one?'

'Noel Maynard.'

Meg sucked in a breath through her teeth. 'That was very unwise of you. Someone should have warned you. He has never really got over that poor girl's murder. He assisted at the autopsy. Can you imagine how that affected him, even after all these years? Now we have to deal with that murderer coming back to live here. Ever since Dr Cooper heard about Maynard's release he's been upset, as indeed we all are.' She gave a little shudder. 'I saw

Maynard the other day and my flesh absolutely crawled. Slinking about town like a mangy dog looking for scraps. God knows he's probably looking for a new victim.'

'I'd better get back to the clinic,' Holly said, glad of a valid excuse to get away.

'I know you meant well, Dr Saxby, but hasn't Dr Cooper suffered enough?'

'Yes...yes, of course... I'm sorry.' Holly made good her escape but it took the rest of the morning before her stomach stopped churning with anguish at the raw pain on Dr Cooper's face when Noel Maynard's name had been mentioned.

CHAPTER TWELVE

WHEN the last patient of the morning had left, Holly informed the receptionist she was going out for a breath of fresh air.

'Are you going anywhere near the General Store?' Sally asked. 'I have some things on order. I might not make it in time this afternoon to pick them up.'

'Sure, I'll do that for you. Is the General Store anywhere near the library?'

'It's on the next block. You can't miss it.'

The librarian didn't bother disguising her surprise at Holly's request to see the newspaper articles that had covered the murder of Tina Shoreham twenty-five years ago. Norma Holden frowned disapprovingly as she handed them to her out of the archive collection. 'They should have given him the death sentence. Jail was too good for him.'

Holly took the folder without commenting. She found a quiet corner and, keeping one eye on the clock, began to read. It was a gruesome story. Tina Shoreham's body had been found in a paddock close to the Maynards' house in the hills, strangled and stabbed. Dr Neville Cooper had assisted with the autopsy. The trial had made national headlines when Noel had been charged with her murder. His blood had been found under Tina's fingernails and, since it was Type A with high levels of copper, indicating Wilson's disease, the case had been wrapped up within a few days upon Noel's confession.

Various accounts documented the locals' hatred of the Maynard boy, who'd had a reputation for being a truant and troublemaker. One witness was quoted as saying that Noel had stalked the victim for months, following her home from school. There was also a photo of the devastated parents, Grant and Lisa, their faces ravaged by grief and shock.

Holly closed the folder and let out a sigh. What a terrible waste. Karen was right. Poor Tina had missed out on living her life, having the experiences most people took for granted. What had been going through Noel's mind to do such a thing? Murderers were made, not born. Had his violent background brought him to it or had there been some other motive?

The same tiny question that had kept her awake the night before kept niggling at the back of her mind.

Her Medline search had come up with only one other known case of an indigenous person with Wilson's disease. Dr Cooper's testing had not been exhaustive by any means. Noel's urine test had turned up some very unusual results for someone with his condition who had not been receiving the correct treatment for nearly two months.

She left the library and went to the General Store and collected Sally's items, but just as she was putting them in her car she noticed the small pharmacy across the road next to the only café. She locked her car and crossed the street. The pharmacist came out of his booth to greet her. 'You must be Dr Saxby.' He stretched out his hand. 'I'm Craig Fulton.'

'Nice to meet you, Craig, and please call me Holly.'

'What can I do for you?' he asked. 'If we haven't got what you want in stock I can order it in for you but it takes a few days, of course.'

'I don't actually need anything at the moment, thank you, but I was wondering if you could do me a small favour?'

'But of course.'

'I was wondering if you could search your database for information on anyone who has had penicillamine dispensed from here in the last twenty-five years.'

He gave her an apologetic look. 'I'm sorry, but our computer files only go back ten years. Before that would be in our record books. It would take months to search through those. I've only been here for the last eight years so I'm not sure I could be much help.'

'Could you find anyone on file who is currently using penicillamine?'

The pharmacist's expression became grim. 'Yes. But you already know who that is because you wrote the prescription for him—Noel Maynard.'

'Yes, that's right. But I was wondering if anyone else had been treated in the past for the same condition.'

'Not with penicillamine, that I can recall. Wouldn't you be better to search through the files at the clinic?' he suggested. 'Dr Cooper was always pretty thorough with keeping notes on his patients. But like here, the computer database won't go back far. You'd have to search through the notes—you'd have a lot of reading to do.'

'Thanks for your help, Craig,' Holly said. 'I'd better get back to the clinic.'

'No problem.'

Holly walked back to her car with a frown. The thought of going through hundreds of patient files by hand was overwhelming. However, the pharmacist had given her something else to ponder. Craig Fulton had said that Dr Cooper had been thorough with keeping patient notes but the file on Noel Maynard was hardly what she would have described as thorough. It wouldn't hurt to have a look through some of his other patient notes to see if what the pharmacist had said was true.

Sally looked up from the desk when she came in with the items from the store. 'Thanks so much for doing that for me. But you shouldn't have hurried back. Your first patient of the afternoon cancelled— her car broke down. You haven't got another one for about twenty minutes.'

'That's fine,' Holly said. 'Could you find some of Dr Cooper's previous patient files for me? I want to familiarise myself with his consultation technique.'

'He was a damn fine doctor,' Sally said as she opened the largest filing cabinet. 'Not much missed his attention. My husband had only gone to him the once and he diagnosed adult-onset asthma. Tim had been breathless for ages but it wasn't until he saw Dr Cooper that the mystery was solved.' She handed a bundle of files over. 'That should keep you busy until the next patient arrives.'

'Thanks.'

Holly took the files to her consulting room and started to flick through each one. Again the handwriting was hard to read but while some of the files were briefer than others, there was no doubt that Dr Cooper had been meticulous in documenting each consultation.

She sat back in her chair and tapped her index finger against her lips. Was his reluctance to document Noel and his family's medical history in similar detail an example of the racism that had been rife at the time? She could imagine that, if so, he would have wanted them out of his consulting room as quickly as possible. Taking copious notes would have only prolonged the consultation.

The intercom buzzed on her desk and Sally told her that the first patient of the afternoon had arrived. Holly gathered the files and took them back out to reception and turned to greet the patient, who was a young man in his twenties with a rather nasty viral infection.

She saw three more patients after him and then another gap appeared in the appointment book. It was too good an opportunity to miss. She turned to Sally, who had just finished taking a message for Cameron.

'I think, rather than sit around waiting, I'll do a

house call. Could you give me some directions to the Maynards' place?'

Sally jerked back in her chair. 'What do you want to go there for? The old lady's just as likely to take a pot-shot at you. And the son... Well, enough said about him. Karen told me she warned you all about him.'

'He's a patient and I'd like to run some more tests on him,' Holly explained. 'He knows he's not welcome in town so I thought I'd make it easier by going to see him. According to the records, Betty Maynard hasn't seen a doctor in years so I think it's high time someone paid her a visit, as well.'

'She's an alcoholic,' Sally said. 'She doesn't need a doctor, she needs a detox clinic.'

'Do you have a map?' Holly asked with a little more forcefulness.

Sally rummaged in the drawer and handed her a crinkled map of the surrounding district. 'You take the road to Baronga Bluff and turn right at the sign marked "Tolly's Hill Lookout". The Maynards' place is the last property on the left. It's not a pretty sight out there. It's little more than a shanty. Not fit for an animal, if you ask me, but then maybe that's just what Noel Maynard is.'

Holly felt herself bristling and without another

word took the map and left, only to cannon into Cameron on her way out the front door of the clinic.

He steadied her with his hands but dropped them as soon as he saw her fiery look. 'Look…about yesterday,' he began.

'Get away from the building!' a now familiar elderly voice roared from just behind them. 'There are land-mines here! Get away, I tell you!'

Holly saw Cameron's eyes roll almost into the back of his head but when he turned to face the old man a smile had taken over his face, his hand raised in a salute. 'How are you, Major Dixon? Fighting fit as usual? Any trouble with the troops today?'

'No, but I want this building cleared immediately,' Major Dixon grumbled. 'It's not safe for civilians. We've already had one casualty.'

Cameron gave the clinic a sweeping glance and turned back to the elderly man. 'You're right, of course. We need to speak to Mayor…er…General Jensen about it. I'll draft an order and have it sent over by runner for you to sign. You'd better get back to base in case you miss it when it's delivered.'

The old man clicked his heels and would have fallen over if Cameron hadn't quickly reached out a hand to steady him. Holly felt a warm sensation pass through her at his respectful gentleness with the senile old man. There was no sign of him making fun of Major Dixon; rather, he treated him as everyone else did—with compassion.

A nurse came out of the nursing home entrance waggling her finger at her charge, exchanging a quick glance with Cameron as she tucked her arm through the major's.

Cameron turned back to Holly once the old man had been escorted safely inside. 'As I was saying, I owe you an apology for my behaviour yesterday. I acted like an out-of-control teenager with a testosterone implant. You should have slapped my face.'

Holly found it hard to hold his gaze. 'It's all right...I shouldn't have insulted you.'

'I probably deserved it.'

'You did.'

He gave a soft chuckle of laughter that sent a ripple of awareness over her skin. To disguise her reaction, she asked him the first question that popped into her head. 'How well do you know Mr Jensen?'

'Clinton's been the town mayor for about four and a half years. He's done a lot for this place. Why do you ask?'

'I had a visit from his stepdaughter yesterday.'

'And?'

'She doesn't sound all that happy at home.'

'She's not the easiest kid to handle,' Cameron admitted. 'She's a moody little thing. Still misses her dad, no doubt. He was killed in a car accident when she was twelve.'

'Do you think there's any possibility she's being abused in some way?'

He frowned down at her. 'That's a very serious allegation, Holly. Did she say something outright or was it just a general impression you got?'

'She didn't say anything outright but she seemed on edge and deeply unhappy.'

Cameron blew out his breath. 'I guess anything's a possibility. But Clinton's the last person I'd suspect of abuse, physical or sexual.'

'Sexual predators can be perfectly normal on the surface,' Holly pointed out. 'That's part of their profile. Married heterosexual men are the worst offenders and no one ever suspects them, which makes it all the harder for victims to speak out about the abuse.'

'I know the stats, but don't you think I would have picked up on something by now? Clinton is a hard-working man who has done his best to raise his son after his first wife died.'

'Jacinta didn't mention anything about a stepbrother.'

'That doesn't surprise me one little bit,' he said. 'She and Martin have never got on. She's as jealous of him as she is of his father. Martin spends most of his time at boarding school in Sydney but he's home for the summer. She's probably reacting to all the attention he's getting. It's very common when a child loses a parent. They become overly attached to the remaining one, which makes future relationships tricky. I wonder how Clinton has put up with it so long.'

'She said she couldn't talk to you because you were a man.'

'A lot of teenage girls are uncomfortable with a male doctor once they hit puberty. I always try to put them at ease but it's been a matter of see me or see no one ever since Dr Cooper had his stroke.'

'I'm not sure what to do about her,' Holly said. 'I suggested she come in and see me with her mother but she didn't seem keen on the idea. I gave her my mobile number in case she changes her mind but I still feel uncomfortable about the whole thing.'

'You did the right thing in giving her your number,' he said. 'If something untoward is going on it gives her a lifeline. You are aware of the proper channels to go through in order to investigate an allegation of abuse?'

'Of course I am,' she said a little tersely.

His gaze went to the map in her hands. 'So where are you off to now?'

'I'm doing a house call. I have some space between patients so I thought I'd call in on Betty Maynard.'

'Noel's mother?' His dark brows met together.

She nodded. 'I checked the records; she hasn't been to a doctor for years, not even you.'

'I visited her when I first came to town but she wasn't keen on unannounced visitors. She pointed a gun at my face until I agreed to never call on her again. I wouldn't go out there without a police escort. The only people she allows anywhere near the place are the Anglican pastor's wife, who drops in her pension and groceries, and the delivery guy from the bottle shop, who keeps her stocked up on gin.'

Holly chewed her lip for a moment. 'I was hoping to ask her about having some tests done.'

'What sort of tests?'

'I've been reading through Noel's history. He was diagnosed with Wilson's disease when he was eighteen and I wanted to check the family history.'

'Wilson's disease?' Cameron's frown increased. 'That's extraordinarily uncommon. Isn't that almost unheard of in an indigenous person?'

'Not completely unheard of. There's one other known case. I checked Medline the other night. When he came to see me the other day he asked for a repeat prescription of penicillamine. He's been on it for years, but he'd been without his medication for the last couple of months, since he's been out of jail. I thought I'd better check his urinary copper levels. The test came back negative.'

'Did you do a blood test? What is it now? Serum something or other, I'd have to look it up.'

'Ceruloplasmin. It should be low. But he wouldn't let me take blood,' she said. 'He was really aggressive about it.'

'You should have told me. I asked if he had given you any trouble and you said no.'

'I didn't want to make a fuss. He obviously has some sort of phobic reaction about needles and blood so I thought it best to leave it for the time being.'

'That must be a first, a murderer who can't stand the sight of blood,' he said dryly.

Holly waited until he brought his gaze back to hers. She let a two beat silence pass before she asked, 'What if he isn't the one who murdered Tina Shoreham?'

Cameron's brows came together again. 'What the hell are you saying?'

'The records Dr Cooper took were sketchy. By today's standards they wouldn't be enough to confirm a diagnosis. You've admitted it yourself. Wilson's disease is extremely rare in an indigenous person. What if it wasn't Noel's blood found under Tina's fingernails? What if it was someone else's, someone who for twenty-five years has got away with her murder?'

CHAPTER THIRTEEN

CAMERON took Holly's arm and led her out of the sun into the shade of a gnarled peppercorn tree. He let her arm go once they were out of the range of the building.

'I don't think you should make those sort of speculations public,' he warned. 'There are people in town who would be outraged by you conducting some sort of campaign to clear Noel Maynard. He was tried by a court of law and found guilty.'

'The law can be an ass, Cameron. What if the evidence was false? What if the doctor got it wrong?'

'Come on, Holly, get real. Dr Cooper was a competent GP who ran this place on his own for thirty-odd years. He was well respected—still is well respected—even though he's now paralysed by a stroke. If there was any mistake made, it's up to the police to check it out. Besides, aren't you forgetting something?'

'What?'

'Noel Maynard pleaded guilty to the murder.'

Holly lowered her gaze a fraction. So too had her cousin pleaded guilty but he still couldn't recall a single event of that fateful night. The police had harangued him, as had his lawyer, insisting he would get off on a lighter sentence if he pleaded guilty. What if Noel had done the same?

'I'd still like to run the tests to make sure he actually has the disease,' she said, bringing her eyes back up to his.

'Fine. But I insist you take someone with you when you call on Betty Maynard. I'll put you in touch with Jean Curtis, the pastor's wife. She can break the ice for you.' He reached into his top pocket and, taking out a pen and a business card, scribbled a phone number on the back of it and handed it to her. 'The rectory is a couple of blocks that way.' He pointed to the end of the street. 'Go and call on her now and introduce yourself. I'll keep an eye on any patients for you until you get back.'

Holly waited until he was back inside the clinic before she started her car and drove it in the direction he'd pointed to. But as she pulled up in front of the rectory she changed her mind about doing as Cameron had advised. Instead she shifted gears and drove on until she found Baronga Bluff Road, and then the turn-off to Tolly's Hill Lookout.

* * *

The Maynard cottage was as Sally had described it. Holly tried not to judge it by her father's Bellevue Hill mansion or her mother and stepfather's Point Piper palace-like terrace, but it was still hard to imagine anyone living here for years on end and, what was more, alone. She parked the car beneath a scraggy gum tree and waited for a sign of anyone moving about. After a few minutes a frail figure appeared at one of the windows.

Holly got out of her car and began to walk towards the house but just as she was about to knock at the door it opened and an elderly woman peered at her through yellowed eyes, a shotgun under one arm.

'What do you want?'

Holly tried to ignore the gun, mentally reassuring herself that it couldn't possibly be loaded. There were strict controls on gun ownership these days and without a supply of bullets she couldn't imagine Noel's mother using it as anything more than a warning to keep strangers away.

'Hello, Mrs Maynard; my name is Dr Holly Saxby. I'm your son's GP. Is he home at present?'

The old woman shook her head. 'He went to town a while back.'

'How long do you think he might be?'

'Half an hour, maybe more.'

'Do you mind if I wait for him here?' she asked.

Betty Maynard's hands trembled on the gun. After a moment or two she put it to one side near the door, shuffled out to the lean-to veranda and indicated for Holly to take one of two old chairs.

Holly sat down gingerly, hoping her Lisa Ho skirt would forgive her for the rough surface. She smiled at the old woman and patted the seat beside her. 'Won't you join me?'

After a small hesitation Betty sat down and stared straight ahead.

'It must be lonely living way out here,' Holly said, filling the uncomfortable silence.

'I don't need people.'

She let another long silence pass. The smell of alcohol was apparent but not quite as apparent as the pungent odour of unwashed skin and hair.

'Noel said you saw him the other day,' the old woman said.

'Yes…I wanted to run some more tests on him.'

'He don't need no more tests done,' Betty said. 'He's got what he's got and there's no changing it.'

'Is there a family history of Wilson's disease?' Holly asked. 'Any other relatives with the same problem?'

'Wouldn't know… I haven't seen any family in a

long time. Not even my daughter, Nell. She took off when Noel was arrested.'

'Have you heard from her lately?'

The old woman shook her head sadly. 'She don't like people to know her brother was charged with murder.'

'You don't think he did it, do you?' Holly asked after another long silence.

'No mother would think her son would do that…but they found his blood on her. He told them he did it.'

'But you still believe he's innocent.'

Betty kept looking into the distance. 'Why would he kill anyone…kill her? She was his friend. Used to come here to visit him. She was trying to help him with his school work. He weren't much good at learning.'

'She came here?'

'Yeah…lots of times.'

'Did her parents know she came to visit Noel?'

'They found out about it. Put a stop to it,' Betty said. 'The day she was killed was the first time she'd come in ages. She must have sneaked out without them knowing.'

Holly felt a shiver pass over her. The poor girl had disobeyed her parents and paid for it with her life. How many teenage girls did the same thing every day? She'd done it herself.

'Mrs Maynard, would you agree to have a blood test? I know you haven't been to a doctor in a long time but I'd like to test you for Wilson's disease.'

'Why?'

'If your son has Wilson's disease he must have inherited it from you and his father. It's inherited; both parents have to have it or at least carry the disease if they don't actually have it. A test will tell us if you're a carrier.'

The old woman appeared to give it some thought. Holly waited patiently, wondering if her quest was going to be successful, when the sound of a bicycle's tyres could be heard crunching over the gravel. She looked up to see Noel pedalling towards them with a bundle of kindling sticks propped under one arm.

He dropped the sticks by the veranda and dusted off his hands, his eyes avoiding hers as he mumbled an almost inaudible greeting. Holly's eyes went to his forearm where one of the sticks had scratched him, the blood already starting to ooze down to his wrist.

'You've cut yourself,' she said. 'I'll get my doctor's bag and tidy it up for you.'

Holly had only taken one step when he looked down at his arm and began to sway on his feet. She watched in alarm as he went as white as anyone with his heritage could go, his legs refusing to hold him upright.

She grabbed him before he fell, pushing his head between his knees and instructing him to take some deep, even breaths.

'That's right,' she said as he got control. 'Nice and deep and even.'

Once she was sure he wasn't going to pass out she left him, dashed to her car and brought her bag back to the veranda. She dressed the wound after applying some betadine, placing the gauze swabs she'd used in a sterile container which she put into her bag.

She straightened. 'There. That should heal in no time. Leave the dressing on for a day or two and try not to get it wet.'

'Thanks,' Noel mumbled without looking at her.

Holly glanced towards her doctor's bag. She couldn't request a genetic test without the patient's permission and she didn't have any paperwork with her.

'Noel—' she turned back to look at him '—would you mind if I came back later with a couple of forms for you to sign? I know you don't want to have a blood test done but the swabs I just used could be enough to trace the genetic abnormality for your Wilson's disease.'

'Why are you doing this?' he asked.

'I got the results back from your urine test,' she said. 'They weren't what I was expecting.'

He looked up at her at that. 'What do you mean?'

'You said you had been without your medication for two months, right?'

'Yeah…' He lowered his gaze to the dusty floorboards on the veranda. 'The prison doctor gave me a prescription but I lost it. I thought I'd wait until I got settled back here to get a new one.'

'A person with Wilson's disease without penicillamine or some other treatment, for that long, should have high levels of copper in their urine. Your tests results came back normal.'

His eyes came back to hers. 'Normal. What does that mean?'

'I'm not sure,' she said, unwilling to commit herself without proof. 'A genetic test could confirm things one way or the other.'

'Are you saying I might not have copper disease?'

'A genetic test could find out for sure.'

His eyes moved away from hers. 'I didn't kill her.'

Holly listened to the sound of the wind moving through the gum trees as she struggled to find something to say. She wanted to believe him but she couldn't be sure if that was because she genuinely thought him incapable of such a crime or whether she was too emotionally involved because of her cousin Aaron.

'Do you remember what happened…that afternoon?' she asked.

He pushed a dead insect away with his foot. 'She came to visit. Rode her bike all the way from town. I told her she shouldn't have come. Her old man was threatening to send her to boarding school if she didn't stay away from me.'

'But she still came to see you.'

He nodded, his expression heart-wrenchingly sad. 'It would have been better for her to go to boarding school…'

'What else did you say to her when she came?'

'Not much…I just walked her back to where she'd left her bike and watched her ride off through the bush.'

'You didn't follow her?'

'No…I didn't have shoes on. Anyway, I didn't want anyone to see me with her, in case her old man got wind of it.'

'And that was the last time you saw her?'

'No…' He stared fixedly at the line in the dust he'd scored with his foot. 'The police showed me photos…'

'You must have found that very upsetting.'

He looked at her once more, the pain in his eyes so stark that Holly felt as if she could feel it reaching out to touch her.

He looked away again. 'That's why I confessed.'

'The photos? You confessed because of those?'

'I couldn't look at them over and over… They thought I was guilty—kept shoving them under my nose… If I just confessed it would stop them doing it… I didn't care what jail would be like. Better place than here once Tina was dead.'

'But Noel, if you didn't kill her, do you have any idea who did do it?'

He shook his head. 'Thought about that a lot the years I was inside. Tina was popular with everyone. Couple of her friends didn't want her spending time with me, but she didn't have any enemies.'

Holly tried to take it all in. It seemed so surreal. Here she was sitting next to a man who had spent twenty-five years in jail for a murder he now said he didn't commit.

He could be lying, a little voice said. *Maybe*, another voice said. *But if he isn't, that means that the person who did kill Tina Shoreham is still at large, maybe still living in Baronga Beach.*

Holly almost jumped out of her skin when she felt a hand touch her on the arm. Betty Maynard gave her an almost toothless smile and offered her arm. 'You can do that blood test if you want.'

Holly gave her a warm smile. 'Thank you, Mrs

Maynard. I'll try and be as gentle as I can but I think we should go inside so Noel doesn't have to watch.'

Holly drove down the road a short time later, glancing worriedly at her car clock. She'd lost track of time and was now over an hour late.

She pulled into the clinic driveway and was just about to enter the building when a man approached her with quick but purposeful strides.

'Dr Saxby?'

'Yes?'

'I'm Clinton Jensen and I'd like a word with you.'

Holly didn't care for his forceful and unfriendly tone. 'I'm sorry, Mr Jensen, but I'm already running late for the clinic. If you'd like to make an appointment, perhaps I could squeeze you in later this afternoon.'

'I don't think you heard me correctly, Dr Saxby. I insist on seeing you now.'

Holly straightened to her full height in heels which, to her immense satisfaction, brought her about two inches above him. 'What is this about, Mr Jensen?'

'I wish to discuss with you the matter of your conversation with my stepdaughter yesterday.'

Holly wasn't sure how to respond. Although he was her stepfather, what she had discussed with Jacinta was not for his ears, but her mother's.

'I'm not sure what you mean.'

'My stepdaughter is a difficult child. I am aware of her tendency to exaggerate certain details. She does it to get attention. Her mother and I are doing our best to keep her on the straight and narrow but she resists all our efforts. She is wilful and disobedient and her coming to see you without our permission only goes to prove it.'

'Surely a girl of fifteen has the right to consult a doctor on her own?'

'Perhaps, but what is discussed during that consultation should be revealed to her legal guardians.'

The ethics of Jensen's point was not so clear-cut—a lot depended on the maturity of the child and what the child had brought up in discussion.

'Why don't you, Mrs Jensen and Jacinta make an appointment with the receptionist and come in and discuss this in the privacy of my consulting room?' she suggested.

'I'm a busy man, Dr Saxby,' he said. 'I've said my piece and I expect you to take note of it. Good day to you.'

Holly watched as he stalked off like a bantam rooster with his feathers in a ruff. She shook her head and turned for the door of the clinic when Major Dixon stopped her.

'I thought I told you, young lady, that this building is out of bounds. Now, move on. *Now!*'

She let out her breath in a frustrated stream. 'Listen, Major, there's a plot afoot to exterminate you. There are snipers everywhere. You'd better take cover before someone takes a pot-shot at you.'

'Snipers?' He narrowed his eyes at her. 'Where?'

She pointed in the direction Clinton Jensen had gone. 'Didn't you see him? He was looking for trouble. I think he's up to no good.'

'Don't worry, Miss, I'll take care of him.' He tottered off over the petunia bed he'd ordered her off—was it only four days ago?

Holly shook her head and entered the clinic. Giving Sally an apologetic glance, she picked up the first file. 'Mrs Trent?' she called to the waiting room.

A middle-aged woman followed her to the consulting room and sat down, her excessive weight making her breathless, and the chair groan.

'What can I do for you, Mrs Trent?'

'I need some more arthritis pills,' she said. 'I'm aching all over.'

'How long have you been on anti-inflammatory medication?' Holly asked, casting her eyes downward for a quick scan of the notes.

'Three years.'

'Have you thought about losing some weight to take the stress off your joints?' she asked. 'Your excess weight is in the morbidly obese range. And that is putting you at risk of deterioration of your joints as well as a host of other diseases such as heart attack, stroke and diabetes.'

'I've tried dieting but it never works long term. I lose a bit, then it creeps back on plus a bit more, no matter what I do. I hardly eat a thing and I'm still overweight.'

'Have you heard of a procedure called lap-banding?'

'I've read about it but I'm not interested. In any case, I don't have private insurance so I could never afford it.'

Holly had heard the same excuses time and again. Statistics showed that most people, predominantly women, spent a couple of thousand dollars on weight-loss programmes with little long-term success, but they baulked at a safe surgical option that cost the same but was effective for life.

'It's worth thinking about,' Holly advised and began to print out a brochure for the patient to read.

While she waited for it to print she took Mrs Trent's blood pressure and jotted down the results in the notes. She handed the brochure over once it came out of the printer.

'Have a read through this information sheet. If you

change your mind I can refer you to an experienced surgeon who does lap-banding. The older surgical options such as stomach stapling and gastric bypass are nowhere near as safe or successful as lap-banding. In the meantime, I'll renew your script for your anti-inflammatory drugs, but I'd like to see you in a week to check your blood pressure again. It's slightly elevated today. I'd like to make sure it's gone back to normal.'

'Thank you,' Mrs Trent said curtly and got to her feet with an effort. 'But if you don't mind, I think I'll go back to seeing Dr McCarrick from now on.'

'Oh?'

'I don't appreciate being told I'm fat,' Mrs Trent said. 'I've never been so insulted in my entire life. You should go back to the city where you belong. This town can do without the likes of you, mixing with those murderous Maynards as bold as you please.'

Holly opened her mouth but clamped it shut again in case she was tempted to speak a little too much of her mind. Mrs Trent waddled out in affront and Holly grimaced when she heard the patient proceed to tell the occupants of the waiting room and the receptionist what had transpired with considerable embellishment on her part. She put her head down on her desk and groaned. Only three hundred and sixty-two days to go.

CHAPTER FOURTEEN

CAMERON found Holly in the kitchenette, still fuming, half an hour later.

'Let me guess—' he gave his stubbly chin a scratch '—a run-in with Maude Trent, right?'

Holly let out a breath of frustration. 'What is it with her? She's morbidly obese, for God's sake! I wouldn't be acting responsibly if I didn't warn her of the health dangers associated with that degree of obesity. She's a stroke or heart attack waiting to happen.'

'True, but there are ways to broach the subject other than hitting her over the head with it.'

She gave him a disparaging glance. 'I did not hit her over the head with it. I raised the problem with her. I suppose you would have found some way of joking about it. Well, sorry, but I don't think it's a laughing matter.'

'You're right, it's nothing to joke about. But you have to understand that as a new doctor in town you have to build up a certain amount of rapport with patients before you hammer them with the truth.'

'How long has she been your patient?'

'She was originally Dr Cooper's patient. I've only been seeing her, and not all that regularly, for the last eighteen months.'

'And has she been in the morbidly obese range all that time?' she asked.

'What exactly is your point?'

'If Mrs Trent had come in to see you about thrush or something and you happened to see a melanoma on her face, would you inform her of it?'

He held her challenging look for a long moment. 'All right. You win. Point taken.'

'Obesity is a huge problem that keeps getting swept under the carpet by patients and doctors. Once a person gets to the morbidly obese range, you know it's virtually impossible to exercise enough to lose the weight, no matter how strict the diet. You realise the current obesity trend in Australia—we're going to have a massive overload on the health system because of all the associated disorders. So why don't you do something about it like any other disease you diagnose?'

'You're preaching to the converted, Holly,' he said. 'I'm well aware of the risks of being overweight.

But, to be fair, Maude Trent is a very lonely woman whose husband left her for a woman half her age and a quarter of her weight. She struggles with depression and I thought it best to broach the subject with tact once we'd established a good doctor-patient relationship. Besides, this is not one of your fancy Northern Sydney suburbs with average incomes running to six figures and everyone in private health insurance. The likes of Maude Trent don't have enough money to put food on the table let alone pay for surgical procedures not covered in the public health system.'

'I beg to differ on whether she has enough money to put food on the table given the current size of her,' Holly shot back without thinking.

Cameron's expression tightened as he looked down at her. 'That's a rather insensitive comment to make, don't you think? And what about her hypothyroidism? Did you happen to read through her notes and see that?'

Holly felt her cheeks storm with colour but pride wouldn't allow her to acknowledge her too hasty and totally unprofessional judgement. 'I haven't had time to read through the whole file yet.'

'Then you should make time before you run off at the mouth. If one of the receptionists heard you, or another patient, it would be all over town within minutes. You'd have no choice but to pack your bags and leave—no one would book in to see you again. Grow up, Holly. Leave your bitchy little comments to silly little schoolgirls and get on with the job you're supposed to be doing—taking care of the whole patient, looking at their whole picture.'

Holly felt herself seething at his tersely delivered put-down. She knew he was right but she hated being dressed down in such a way. It reminded her too much of her father—always insisting on winning every argument, making her feel stupid and incompetent in the process.

'You have no right to speak to me that way,' she bit out.

'I have every right to ensure you follow the professional code of this practice, which happens to include not insulting patients, to their faces or behind their backs. I've already had a phone call from Clinton Jensen a short time ago. He said you were unspeakably rude to him in the car park in full hearing of passers-by. You'll have to get your attitude sorted out or I'll have to recommend the Regional Health Board rethink their decision to hire you.'

She glared at him in outrage. 'You wouldn't dare!'

His eyes glittered as they held hers challengingly.

'Just watch me, sweetheart.' He put his used coffee cup down on the nearest surface with a clunk and brushed past her, clipping the door shut behind him.

Holly clenched her fists by her sides in an effort to control her rage. She knew he would do it. And with that sort of black mark on her CV it would have an effect on every job she ever applied for in the future. Besides, she could hardly pack up and leave now. She'd rented out her apartment for the whole year to a friend of a friend from medical school, and staying with either of her parents and their current partner was totally out of the question.

Her shoulders slumped in resignation. It looked like another chunk of humble pie had to be eaten and every single mouthful was going to choke her, she was sure.

When Holly went back out to reception Sally informed her that she had no other patients for the day.

'Are you sure?' She peered over the receptionist's shoulder to look at the appointment book.

Sally sat back in her chair with her arms folded across her ample chest. 'Three cancelled and the other four have switched to see Dr McCarrick.'

Holly chewed her bottom lip as Sally turned to speak to a tall middle-aged man who'd just come in.

'Hello, Mr Cooper.' Sally gave him a friendly

smile. 'I didn't know you were coming to town this week. Have you been to visit your father?'

Holly pricked up her ears at the mention of the name Cooper.

'Yes,' the man answered. 'And I'm extremely annoyed about a visit he had today from the new doctor in town.'

Holly wished she could sink through the carpet and disappear beneath the floorboards.

'Well, you're in luck,' Sally said, glancing at Holly. 'Here she is right now.'

Holly stepped from behind the reception desk and offered her hand. 'Hello, Mr Cooper. I'm Dr Holly Saxby.'

The man ignored her hand and bit out through clenched teeth, 'I'd like a word with you. In private.'

Holly had never actively wished for an acute emergency before, but judging by the look of fury in Dr Cooper's son's eyes, surely a code blue would be preferable to facing such rage.

'Come through to my office,' she said, a little annoyed with herself for sounding so intimidated.

He didn't bother to sit down when she offered him a chair in her room. Instead he glowered down at her, his face almost puce. 'I would like to know what you think gives you the right to upset my father the way you did this morning. I received a call from the nursing home earlier today to inform me that you had upset him by asking him questions you had no business asking.'

'I'm sorry, Mr Cooper, but as your father once treated a patient of mine I thought it appropriate to ask his advice.'

'*His advice?*' he blustered. 'It sounds to me you made suggestions of malpractice. I am a lawyer, and there would be grounds for legal proceedings.'

Holly felt her stomach cave in with panic. God, what had she done? This was only day four—so far she'd wrecked her knee and nearly drowned, Cameron was threatening to have her contract revoked, the mayor and Maude Trent were intent on ruining her credibility, and now Dr Cooper's son was threatening a legal suit against her. Could it get any worse?

'I'm very sorry that I upset your father, Mr Cooper,' she said meekly. 'I did not know how intimately involved with…the murder case he'd been. As you know, I'm only new in town. I haven't had time to take stock of everything. I was just trying to sort out an inconsistency in a patient's history, that's all. I really didn't mean to imply anything untoward about your father. He is greatly respected in this town and I hope you will accept my apology for causing any hurt to him, or to you.'

She held her breath but after a lengthy pause she heard Mr Cooper release a sigh.

'Thank you for your apology,' he said. 'My father is very frail and not expected to live much longer. I hate the thought of anyone upsetting him at this delicate stage of his life. I want his last days to be as peaceful as possible.'

'I understand…' She captured her bottom lip momentarily.

He held out his hand. 'I'm Geoffrey, by the way.'

She tentatively shook his hand. 'I really am very sorry, Mr…I mean Geoffrey.'

'I'm not really going to sue you,' he said, smiling for the first time.

Holly did her best to hide her relief but she couldn't quite help a tiny wry smile. 'My father is a barrister so it would've been rather embarrassing for me if you had.'

'Is he really?' His brows rose slightly. 'What firm?'

'Saxby Sentinelle and Smithton.'

'Impressive.'

'Yes, well, he certainly seems to think so.'

He gave a short chuckle of laughter but Holly couldn't help feeling it was a little forced—nothing like the deep amused rumble of Cameron's that had sent her stomach into a tailspin so often.

'I'll be in town for a couple of days,' he said into the little silence that had fallen. 'Let's put this behind us, then. I would be honoured if you would consider having a drink with me this evening. Perhaps around seven? I'm staying at the hotel as my father's house was sold a few months ago.'

Holly wanted to refuse, but after Cameron's dressing down earlier she was feeling the need to restore some remnant of her tattered feminine self-confidence. Geoffrey Cooper wasn't exactly her type, but now that he was clearly making an effort to alleviate the situation she saw no reason to decline the invitation. Besides, if there were any other repercussions from her visit to his father this might be one way of avoiding them.

'That would be very nice, thank you,' she said. 'I haven't been to the hotel yet. What is it called?'

'The Plover's Rest,' he said. 'Shall I meet you there or would you like me to pick you up?'

'I'll meet you there,' she said with a friendly smile.

Holly was already running late for her date when there was a knock at the front door of the cottage. She had lost an hour going back to the Maynards' place for the patient authority form to be signed by Noel and had only just had time for a quick freshen up.

She muttered a little curse and put her wand of mascara down. She slipped her feet into her heels and, giving her upswept hair a little glance on the way past the mirror in the hall, opened the door.

'Oh, it's you.'

'Nice to see you, too,' Cameron said. 'Can I come in?'

She shifted from foot to foot. 'Actually, I'm in kind of a hurry.'

'Where are you going?'

She gave him an imperious look. 'On a date.'

Something intangible shifted behind the wall of Cameron's chest. He hoped she didn't see the flicker of it in his eyes when he asked, 'With whom?'

'Geoffrey Cooper. He's asked me out for a drink.'

'Lucky Geoffrey.' He rocked back on his heels as his green-blue gaze ran over her slim-fitting outfit and impossibly high heels. 'But do you think you should be stressing that knee of yours with those heels?'

'I think I'll survive one drink at the hotel without stressing it too much,' she answered.

'One drink, eh?' He curled his lip. 'Is that all he's asked you out for?'

She placed one hand on her hip and gave him a haughty look. 'So far.'

'Batteries finally run out, have they?' He knew he shouldn't have said it but it was almost worth it to see the way her cheeks instantly flamed. She was so damned cute he could hardly stand it. Her glossed lips were pouting and her perfume was reaching out to him in intoxicating waves.

'I wish you would stop referring to that… that…that device,' she said. 'It was a ridiculous going-away gift from the girls at the Mosman clinic—a joke. That's surely something you would understand given your propensity to find humour in every situation.'

'You take life far too seriously, Holly. But I'm not here to tell you that.'

She let out a sigh of boredom. 'So why are you here?'

Cameron found it hard not to drag her into his arms and kiss that provocative pout away, but somehow he resisted the impulse. 'I wanted to check that you were OK. I heard some of your patients cancelled at the last minute.'

'I hardly see that it's any concern of yours.'

'It can be difficult being the new kid on the block and being excluded from all the games.'

'I'm sure I'll survive. Now, if you'll excuse me, I

really must get ready for my date.' She tried to close the door but he put his foot in the way.

'No, wait,' he said. 'There's one other thing.'

Her hands fell away from the door to fold across her chest. Cameron had to wrench his gaze away from what the action did to her cleavage, but even so his groin gave him a pulsing reminder of how much she affected him. It was totally out of character for him but he couldn't seem to control his reaction to her every time she was near. It had taken months of long-distance dating with Lenore for him to feel ready to take things to the next stage and yet he'd known Holly barely a couple of days and he wanted her in his arms—for ever.

'I was wondering…if you'd like to have dinner with me tomorrow night.' It was the first thing to come into his head and by the reaction on her face it was quite possibly the last thing she'd expected him to say.

She gave him a narrow-eyed look. 'I thought you were going to have me reported to the Regional Board as incompetent? Is dinner with you some sort of softening up process before you deliver the final blow?'

'I have no intention of reporting you to the Regional Board. You just got under my skin this afternoon, that's all. It was just a throw-away line.'

'Well, try this on for a throw-away line.' She gave the door another savage nudge against his foot. 'You can take your dinner invitation and shove it up your—' Holly had every intention of finishing her sentence but his mobile went off just before she got to the best bit. She watched as he took it from his belt and answered it, his brow furrowing as he listened to the voice on the other end.

'When?' he asked. 'Is she all right?'

Holly found herself straining her ears to pick up what she could of the conversation but it was hard to make out what was being said with any accuracy, although Cameron's expression seemed to imply that it was something serious. He ended the call and confirmed her fears.

'You'd better cancel your date,' he said grimly. 'That was Jacinta Jensen's mother. Apparently Jacinta was attacked earlier this afternoon. She's only just told her mother and stepfather. They're going to meet us at the clinic in five minutes.'

CHAPTER FIFTEEN

'DID she tell her parents who attacked her?' Holly asked as they made their way out to Cameron's car, her heart thudding with alarm.

'Yes, she did.' He gave her a sobering look as he unlocked the vehicle. 'Noel Maynard. Rob Aldridge, the local cop, is on his way out there now to bring him in for questioning. He wanted to make sure he had Noel in custody before he took a statement from Jacinta in case he went into hiding.'

Holly strapped on her seatbelt with hands that were visibly shaking. How could she have been so easily duped? Noel's act as the interned innocent had been so convincing, but even still she was annoyed with herself for falling for it so readily.

'Still think he's innocent?' Cameron threw her a quick glance once they were on their way.

'I was only speculating,' she defended herself.

'Those test results threw me a bit but I've since organised genetic testing.'

'How did you manage that? I thought he refused to have a blood test?'

'When I went out there to visit his mother he had a scratch on his arm so I dressed it for him and asked his permission to use the swab for the test.'

'I thought I told you not to go out there alone.'

'I didn't want to waste time introducing myself to the pastor's wife. I thought it would be quicker just to go straight there.'

He angled his gaze at her once more. 'Did he tell you how he got the scratch?'

'No, but since he was carrying a bundle of sticks for kindling I assumed he'd done it on one of them.'

'The Maynards, just like everyone else out at Tolly's Hill Lookout, have electricity connected,' he said as he pulled into the clinic car park. 'And it's the middle of summer, and there's a total fire ban in place. Didn't you think it a bit unusual for him to be carting firewood about?'

Holly chewed her bottom lip as she thought about her oversight. When she'd gone inside with Betty to take her blood for the test she hadn't noticed a fuel stove of any sort. She'd noticed an electric stove and cook-top but no sign of anything that would require firewood.

'No…no, I didn't…'

'What time did he come back from town?' he asked as he led the way inside. 'Try and be as accurate as you can so Rob can profile his movements in case Maynard comes up with an alibi.'

'It was mid afternoon, about three, I think.'

Valerie Dutton came through the front door to greet them. 'She's in your consulting room with her mother and stepfather, Dr McCarrick. I thought it would be more private than the cubicles next door.'

'Good thinking,' Cameron said and led the way through.

'Oh, thank God you could come!' Renee Jensen cried, her face ravaged by tears. 'Look what that animal has done to my daughter!'

Holly looked at the slumped figure of Jacinta sitting in one of the chairs, quietly sobbing. She had a black eye and the tops of her arms were heavily marked with bruises as if someone had dug their fingertips in savagely.

Cameron squatted down in front of her but she turned away as if she couldn't bear to look at him and started sobbing all the harder. He exchanged a quick glance with Holly as he straightened, then, turning to Clinton and Renee, took them to one side. 'I think it might be best if we let Dr Saxby talk to

Jacinta. This has been a terrifying ordeal and we don't have a female police officer in town. It might be better to let Holly handle this. Let's go out and wait for Rob Aldridge to arrive. He shouldn't be much longer.'

'We'd rather stay, if you don't mind,' Clinton Jensen said.

'I don't want *you* here.' Jacinta scowled at her stepfather.

'Listen here, young lady, that is no way to speak to your—'

'You're not my father!' she cried. 'I hate you and your stupid son. I hate you! I wish you'd never come into our lives.'

'Jacinta!' Renee Jensen gasped. 'How can you say that after all Clinton has done for you?'

Cameron took Jacinta's mother and stepfather each by the arm and led them out of the room, doing his best to reassure them as he went. 'Dr Saxby will be able to handle this a whole lot better if we get out of the way. Come and I'll make you both a cup of tea and you can tell me your side of this afternoon's events.'

Holly waited until they had gone before pulling over a chair and placing it close to Jacinta's. 'Jacinta, do you feel up to telling me what happened?'

The young girl buried her head in her hands and

began to sob again. 'He grabbed me and tried to kiss me. I thought he was going to kill me.'

Holly felt a wave of nausea pass through her. It seemed unbelievable that such a short time ago she had been sitting chatting to Noel Maynard when she'd taken the forms out to him to sign.

'Did you see his face?'

Jacinta kept her head in her hands. 'Yes.'

'Enough to give the police a good description?'

She nodded without lifting her head from her hands.

Holly tried to recall the sexual assault procedure she'd been taught. 'Do you mind if I examine your injuries, Jacinta? I promise to be very gentle. You've had a terrible shock and it can be very traumatic recalling what happened, so only tell me what you feel comfortable telling me, OK?'

The young girl lifted her head out of her hands but didn't quite meet Holly's gaze. There was nothing unusual in that, Holly reminded herself. Victims of sexual assault were often filled with shame at what had happened to them.

'I don't need examining,' Jacinta said. 'He didn't do anything…sexual. He just…grabbed me and hit me in the face…' She began to cry again.

'Did he threaten you in any other way?' Holly asked gently once Jacinta's sobs had subsided a little.

'Yes… He said if I told anyone he was going to…k-kill me.'

'How did you manage to escape?'

'I scratched him with my hands,' she said.

Holly looked down at the girl's well-bitten finger-nails. 'Have you washed your hands since he attacked you?'

Jacinta nodded. 'I had a shower and scrubbed myself all over. I felt dirty and ashamed of him touching me.'

Textbook reaction, Holly noted grimly. It was a wonder she'd reported the attack at all. So many victims didn't.

'You did the right thing reporting this, Jacinta. I know it's hard for you but it means the police can stop this happening to someone else. The police officer will have to take a formal statement from you so charges can be laid.'

Jacinta started to worry her bottom lip with her teeth.

Holly held her breath. This was also textbook—the last-minute rethink about laying charges. The judicial system had had a complete overhaul in recent years over the handling of sexual assault cases but it was still a harrowing experience and far too many victims pulled the plug at the last minute.

'Your mum will support you no matter what, Jacinta,' she said reassuringly.

'I don't want to go through with this.' Jacinta got to her feet in agitation. 'I can't. I just can't.'

'But whoever did this to you must be brought to justice,' Holly said. 'You said you can positively identify him. That's all the police need to begin the process. He hurt you, Jacinta. You have a black eye and bruises all over your arms. It could have been much worse and if you don't follow through on this he could do it to someone else, maybe even one of your friends.'

'Please…' Jacinta was almost hysterical. 'I want to go home. I don't want to talk to the police. I don't want to lay charges. Let me go home!'

The door burst open and Renee Jensen came in with her arms outstretched to embrace her daughter. 'Don't worry, poppet. I'm here now.' She gave Holly a quelling look over her daughter's head. 'I won't let the doctor upset you any more.'

'Mrs Jensen, I—'

'I know all about you,' Renee Jensen snarled. 'The whole town is talking about it. You don't think he did it, do you? You don't think Noel Maynard killed Tina Shoreham and now you've convinced my daughter not to report what he did to her. Look at her, for God's sake! She's been brutalised by that murdering monster and you're doing nothing about it!'

Cameron had followed Mrs Jensen in with her husband. 'Renee, this is not helping anything,' he said. 'Why don't you take Jacinta home and if she feels up to speaking to Rob Aldridge later on then that can be arranged.' He turned to Clinton. 'Take them both home, Clinton. Call me if you have any worries during the night.'

He turned to Holly once they'd left. 'I take it she wasn't very cooperative?'

Holly let out a defeated sigh. 'I thought I was handling it so well but as soon as I mentioned laying charges she became hysterical.'

'The thought of facing your attacker in court is daunting,' he said. 'Did she give you any details of what happened?'

'Not much…I didn't want to push for too much in case it upset her but she said nothing sexual happened other than he tried to kiss her. He hit her on the face which blackened her eye and I assume the bruises on her arms are from where he grabbed her. She said he threatened to kill her if she told anyone. I guess that's why she left it so late to tell her mother.' She let out another sigh. 'She said she'd scratched him in self-defence but she's showered since the attack so there was no sign of blood under her already chewed-to-the-elbow nails.'

'So it's her word against his.'

'I guess so…'

Cameron glanced at his watch. 'Did you call your date to tell him you couldn't make it?'

She put her hands to her face and gasped. 'I completely forgot! He must think I stood him up or something.'

'It's only just gone eight. I'll drop you off on my way home.'

'Oh, do you mind?' She gave him a grateful look.

Yeah, I do, actually, Cameron thought. *I hate the thought of someone else looking into those melting-chocolate eyes. I hate the thought of someone else kissing that beautiful mouth and I hate the thought of someone else thinking of a way to get her to sleep with them.* Damn it! He wanted to make love to her, had wanted to from the first moment she had looked down her cute little nose at him and told him off. He hadn't thought it possible to fall in love again after what Lenore had done to him but something about Holly had got under his guard. She was a delightful mixture of sassiness and self-doubt. He liked that about her. Lenore had been so full of confidence; nothing had ever dented it, not even when he'd first told her he wouldn't consider living in the city. She had smiled at him smugly, confident she would eventually change his mind. She'd dismissed his convictions as if they meant nothing. Holly, on the other hand, in spite of her bad feeling towards him, had come to him and expressed her apology so sweetly it had rocked him to the core. Somehow he felt sure if she made up her mind to do something she would see it through no matter what. Her first three days in town had been nothing short of disastrous, but here she was, still going in to bat.

'He might not have waited for you,' he said.

'I know…' She gave her bottom lip a little nibble. 'I didn't think to get his number off him but I know he's staying at the hotel so I can at least leave a message.'

'Do you want me to wait in case he isn't there?' Cameron said a short time later as he pulled up in front of The Plover's Rest.

'I don't want to put you out…'

'It's no trouble,' he assured her. 'What say I give you ten minutes and if he doesn't show then at least I'll be here to take you home?'

'All right…if you're sure…'

He smiled even though it hurt him. 'Go and have a good time. It's been a tough few days, you deserve some chill-out time.'

He watched her totter into the hotel in her ridiculously high heels. She was doing her best to disguise her limp but it only made him admire her more. Lenore would have milked her injury for all it was worth, insisted on being waited on hand and foot.

He let out a deep sigh and, closing his eyes, leaned his head back against the headrest. He'd give her twenty minutes and after that he would go home…

CHAPTER SIXTEEN

HOLLY rushed into the hotel but the bar was almost empty apart from two men propping up the counter. There was no sign of Geoffrey and when she asked for the barman who doubled as the accommodation receptionist to call his room he informed her that Mr Cooper had left for Sydney more than half an hour ago.

'Are you sure?' she asked with a worried look.

The barman nodded as he poured another Scotch for the elder of the men. 'Here you go, Fred, but you'd better make it your last. I don't want you getting into any trouble. Remember the last time. Rob Aldridge had to let you sleep it off in the lock-up.'

The man mumbled something in reply and tossed the Scotch down his throat before he turned to look at Holly. His mouth curled up in a sneer as he addressed her. 'So, you're the new doctor who thinks Noel Maynard's innocent.'

Holly felt herself stiffening as she met his mocking gaze. 'I don't recall saying as such publicly.'

'You don't have to in a place like Baronga Beach,' the man said with another smirk. 'You have only to think it and it's the next day's news.' He leaned a little closer, the strong alcohol fumes wafting over her face as he added in a chilling undertone, 'Better be careful, missy. There's people in town who don't like things said that shouldn't be said or even thought about, for that matter. It could get very unpleasant for you around here, if you know what I mean.'

Holly tightened her mouth and turned and left before she was tempted to respond.

She made her way out to the car park and tapped on the driver's window of Cameron's car. He jerked awake and looked at her bleary-eyed.

'Is that offer of a lift still on?' she asked.

He rolled down the window. 'What happened? Did he stand you up?'

'No.' She found herself lying to him for the sake of her flagging pride.

He glanced down at his watch. 'Is this what they call speed-dating? You've been five minutes, tops.'

'It's amazing what you can find out about a person in five minutes,' she said with a pointed look.

He held her fiery gaze for a moment, a small smile

playing around his mouth before he jerked his head towards the passenger door. 'Come on, get in.'

She stalked around to the passenger side and climbed in, snapping the door shut.

'So, how was Geoffrey Cooper this evening—full of himself as usual?'

She pulled down the seatbelt without answering.

'Like that, huh?'

She turned her head to glare at him. 'What do you mean, "like that, huh"? What's "huh"? I arranged to have a drink with him. Is that against the law or something?'

'He didn't ask to see you again?'

She folded her arms across her chest and wished she hadn't backed herself into a corner by lying to him in the first place. 'No.'

'Maybe his conscience gave him a little prick. God knows it's about bloody time.'

She turned to look at him. 'What do you mean?'

He sent her a sideways glance. 'Did he happen to mention during your five-minute date that he's married?'

Holly's stomach gave a vertiginous lurch. '*Married?*'

'His wife's name is Gillian. Nice lady, if you have a thing for loud-spoken, brassy, busty blondes.'

Holly didn't speak again until he'd pulled into his driveway. 'Thank you for the lift,' she said somewhat stiffly. 'I didn't expect you to wait for me.'

He gave her a twinkling grin. 'I had nothing better to do and it was only five minutes, after all.'

She got out of the car but he followed her right to her door.

'Wait, Holly,' he said when she put her key in the lock.

'Go away.' She gave him a little push but it was like trying to shove away concrete. Her hand connected with his hard abdomen and bounced off. '*Ouch!*' She flapped her hand. 'I think you've broken my fingers.'

'Let me see.'

'No!' She snatched her burning hand out of his grasp and, fumbling with her key, unlocked the door.

Cameron saw it first and did his best to block her vision but it was too late. She had slipped out of his hold and was now staring at the bloodied mess on the floor right in front of her.

'Oh, my God...' She stepped backwards in horror, her heart leaping to her throat, her stomach tripping in panic.

He pulled her back from the macabre sight of blood spattered all over the newly painted walls of the hall.

Feathers from a dead chicken were all around the room. There was message scrawled on one wall.

You will be next.

'Oh, my God...' She grasped at his arms for support, her legs wobbling in shock. 'Oh, my God...'

'It's all right, Holly.' He backed out of the cottage, taking her with him. 'It's just a stupid practical joke.'

She gave him a hard shove, her heart still racing with the aftermath of fear. 'How could you?'

He looked at her incredulously. 'You think I did that?'

She gave him an accusing glare. 'Didn't you?'

'Of course not! For God's sake, what sort of man do you think I am?' He ran a hand through his hair distractedly.

'Who else has a key to this cottage?'

He frowned down at her. 'No one, apart from me.'

'So can you explain why a decapitated chicken is lying in my hall, because if you can't there must be someone else in town who has a key and an equally sick sense of humour.' She gave another shiver and rubbed at the still prickling skin of her upper arms.

'Holly, surely you don't think—'

'I don't know what to think!' she cried, her eyes wide with fear. 'I'm not a vegetarian but if I have to see that sort of thing again I might very well turn into one. Who would do such a thing?'

'I don't know.' He pulled her towards his cottage next door. 'But we need to get you out of the way of whoever is behind this.' He unlocked the front door and ushered her in, closing the door behind him.

Holly felt a shiver pass through her at the grim look on his face. She tried not to cry but she felt perilously close to it. 'Y-you think someone is trying to scare me?'

'It looks that way.'

She suddenly recalled the man at the bar and his thinly veiled warning.

Cameron frowned as he saw her expression. 'What is it?'

'There was a man in the bar... He spoke to me about Noel Maynard.'

'What did he say?'

'He said there were people in town who would make things unpleasant for me if I went around claiming Noel's innocence.'

'Who was it?'

'I think his name was Fred.'

'Did Geoffrey hear the conversation?'

Holly gave him a shamefaced look. 'Geoffrey wasn't there.'

'He'd already left?'

'He wasn't there at all,' she confessed with a little sigh. 'I guess he got tired of waiting for me. The barman said he'd left for Sydney half an hour or so earlier.'

Cameron quietly processed what she'd just told him. Geoffrey Cooper was hardly more than a passing acquaintance but he certainly had been very angry about Holly's visit to his father that afternoon. Sally had told him how he'd come to the clinic and torn strips off Holly, not caring who heard him. But surely with Geoffrey's legal background he wouldn't go as far as to leave such a grisly warning in her cottage. Of course, it could have been Fred Blaney himself, but then why would he go out of his way to warn her when by doing so the finger of blame would immediately point to him? It just didn't make sense. Fred liked a drink and had a bit of a temper at times, but he wasn't a total fool.

'Look, you'll be safe here,' he said, doing his best to reassure her. 'I'll give Rob Aldridge a call and get him to take a look. But in the meantime, you'd better stay with me overnight.'

'Here?' Holly looked around at the half-finished

sitting room. There were paint tins and splash sheets all over the floor and a ladder propped against the wall.

'I know it's not quite your usual five-star standard but at least there are no slaughtered chickens under the bed.'

She disguised another shudder and asked, 'And exactly where is the bed?'

'Where do you think it is?' He pressed rapid dial on his phone. 'It's in my bedroom.'

'Is that another one of your stupid jokes?'

'I'm not joking, Holly. I only have one bed but it's big enough for both of us.'

'I'm not sleeping with you!'

He held up his hand to shush her as he had a brief word with the local cop. 'Yeah, Hi, Rob. I've got a situation here you might want to take a look at.' Holly listened as he gave a cut-down version before he added, 'It's not a pretty sight... Right, I'll meet you there in five minutes.' He clipped his phone back on his belt. 'Rob's on his way. Come through and I'll show you where the bathroom is and once Rob and I have cleaned up next door I'll take you back for some of your things.'

'Do you really think this is necessary?' she asked, desperately trying to put on a brave front but not sure she was being very successful. Her heart was still thumping irregularly and her stomach felt cold and hollow. 'I'm sure whoever did that is hardly going to risk being caught having another attempt to scare me at this time of night.'

'Listen, Holly. Whoever did this is very determined to unnerve you. Rob agrees you should stay with me tonight. It could just be a joke but what if it isn't? Who knows what else this sick person has in their repertoire?'

Holly couldn't quite suppress another little shudder. It just didn't bear thinking about.

'I'll just have a quick run through in here to see that everything's secure before I meet Rob next door.'

'*Wait!*' She bolted after him, almost cannoning into his back in her haste. He turned and steadied her and, slipping his warm fingers around hers, gave her hand a little squeeze. 'Come on then, stay close while I make sure no one's added to the colour scheme here.'

Holly stayed by his side as he inspected each room but, apart from the kitchen, the place was such a mess she couldn't see anyone wasting their time adding to the mayhem.

She said as much to Cameron. 'This place looks as if a bomb hit it. Do you have a thing about tidying up after yourself?'

'I know exactly where everything is.'

She gave a cynical little grunt as she stepped over a pile of unfolded clothes on the floor when he pulled her with him into his bedroom.

'What?' He looked down at her.

'What is it with men and housework?' she asked. 'Or are you waiting for some poor woman to come along and take over where your mother left off?'

'What is it with women and obsessive tidiness?' he clipped back. 'I'm a busy man. I don't have time to fold and iron clothes ahead of time. I only do them as I need them.'

Holly's eyes went to the bed. The white Egyptian cotton linen certainly looked very clean but the quilt and pillows looked as if he'd thrown them haphazardly back on the bed after tumbling out that morning. She could even see the creases on one of the pillows where his head had lain.

A funny sensation made its way across the bottom of her belly at the thought of him lying sprawled in that big bed, his long tanned limbs stretched out, his naked body unashamedly on show...

She pulled away from where her traitorous thoughts were leading, more than a little shocked at herself for allowing her increasing attraction to him to take over her common sense. What was she thinking? It wasn't as if she really even liked him.

Well, maybe a bit...

She thought about the way he'd tried to protect her from seeing that ghastly chicken, his clean male smell filling her nostrils, his arms strong and steady as they held her trembling figure.

Mmm... Maybe she liked him more than a little bit, more like a lot...

'Make yourself comfortable and I'll be back as soon as I've finished with Rob,' he said. 'And don't answer the door.'

Holly let out a little sigh once he'd gone. Was it crazy to be in love with someone after only four days? It had taken her months to fall in love with Julian and even then... Well, *of course* she'd been in love with him...a bit.

Her frown increased as she tried to push the truth away but it just wouldn't go. The truth was she had been in love with the idea of being secure in a relationship. She hadn't truly been in love with Julian at all. Not the sort of love that would last. Not the sort of love that would make her think about spending the rest of her life in the country with a man who had convictions so strong they only made her admire and love him even more.

But so far her foray into the country was turning out to be a total nightmare. And she'd thought the inner city streets of Sydney were dangerous! At least no one had ever sacrificed a hapless hen on her doorstep.

For something to do other than brood she started to straighten the bed. She was a neat-nik from way back, ever since her parents had divorced. She'd had two houses to move between so it had become somewhat of an obsession to have things super-organised to avoid the panic of not having what she needed for the next day at school. Cameron could scoff all he liked, but she liked order around her. It made her feel secure when other things in her life were not. And right now things weren't feeling too secure.

Once the bed was made she started on the pile of clothes on the floor, folding each article into neat little piles—socks, shorts, jeans, shirts and... Her stomach did another little shuffle when she picked up a pair of his underpants. She quickly folded them and put them beside his socks.

She chewed the end of her finger when all the clothes were sorted. What was she supposed to do now?

Her gaze went to the cluttered surface of a chest of drawers. It was littered with papers and receipts, loose coins and a collection of framed photographs. She went closer to inspect the photos, picking up the first one.

It was a childhood shot of Cameron and his family,

his older brother and younger sister on either side of him and his parents at each end. Her heart tightened at the liveliness, mischievousness and affection that shone from each family member's eyes. She couldn't help wondering how they had coped with the subsequent loss of their son and brother. How indeed did anyone cope?

It seemed ages before she heard the sound of Cameron's voice calling out to let her know he was back. She carefully put the frame down and came out to the kitchen where he introduced her to the close-to-retirement police officer who had followed him in. Once the introductions were out of the way Rob Aldridge began to take a statement from her. After she'd told him what she could, including what Fred Blaney had said, he looked up from his note taking. 'So you have no idea of anyone else who would want to threaten you?'

She shook her head in bewilderment. 'I've only been in town three days, four if you include Sunday afternoon when I first arrived.'

'What about Noel Maynard? He's your patient now, right?'

'Yes, but I don't think…' She stopped when she saw the hardened cynicism in his eyes.

'He's killed before, Dr Saxby, and only this afternoon he attacked a teenage girl. Don't be fooled by him. It's clear he's fooled the prison psychiatrist who assured the authorities he had zero likelihood of re-offending. I was unable to bring him in for an interview. He's flown the coop, so to speak.'

'Oh…'

'I've asked for someone from Jandawarra to come up and help me track him down, but until we find him I want you to stay with Dr McCarrick.'

'There are probably other people besides Mr Maynard who could just as easily have done this to scare me,' Holly said. 'It might not be him at all.'

'Perhaps, but whoever it is, it certainly seems you've made an enemy in town,' he observed. 'That is unless someone has followed you here.'

She looked at him in growing consternation. 'What do you mean?'

'You've just moved down from the city, right? Have you had a recent break-up with a boyfriend that might have caused him to try and get back at you?'

'You mean like stalking me or something?'

'Yeah, it happens all the time, ex-partners who just won't let go. It's a real problem these days.'

Holly almost laughed out loud at the thought of Julian Drayberry stalking her in an attempt to get her to come back to him. 'I don't think my ex-fiancé's new wife would allow him out of her sight long enough for him to make a phone call to me, let alone orchestrate a terror campaign.'

Cameron frowned as he listened to the exchange. He hadn't realised her ex-fiancé had married someone else so quickly. No wonder she was so uptight and lacking in confidence. Her self-esteem had taken the biggest knock of all. He should know—it had taken him this long to get over his own relationship disaster.

'Well, if you think of anything significant, let me know,' Rob said. He turned to Cameron. 'I'll see myself out. I'll have another look around outside before I head off.'

'Thanks.'

Holly rubbed her upper arms again once the police officer had left. 'This is really creeping me out. I thought the country was supposed to be quiet and boring. What is it with this place?'

'It's normally the quietest place on earth but for some reason ever since you turned up everything's gone haywire,' he said.

'So you think it's my fault?'

'Rob's right, Holly. I know you've only been here a short time but you've certainly upset someone . The question is, who would be at the top of that list?'

She rolled her eyes in disdain. 'You're making me sound like some sort of social misfit, as if I can't make a single friend.'

He gave her a long and thoughtful look. 'You have made a couple of friends but the rest of the towns-folk don't approve.'

'You mean Noel Maynard and his mother?'

He nodded. 'I warned you that people wouldn't take too kindly to you springing to a convicted killer's defence. Sally told me about Geoffrey bawling you out in reception about your visit to his father. What on earth did you say to him to bring his son down here in such a tearing hurry?'

'He thought I'd made accusations of malpractice against his father. But once I'd apologised and told him I hadn't actually said that at all, he calmed down. That's why he asked me to meet him for a drink—to make amends for shouting at me.'

'But he didn't turn up as arranged.'

His contemplative tone brought Holly's eyes back to his. 'You think Geoffrey's responsible for the chicken?'

He gave a non-committal shrug and asked, 'Who phoned him and told you had visited his father?'

'I don't know… One of the nurses, perhaps.'

'Did anyone overhear your conversation with Neville Cooper?'

'It was hardly what I'd call a two-way conversation,' Holly said. 'The poor man can barely say a word. He got upset when I mentioned Noel Maynard's name and when I had a chat with the nurse on duty, someone called Meg, she said it was because he'd been at the autopsy on Tina Shoreham and even after all this time it still upsets him.'

'That stands to reason,' he said, rubbing his jaw thoughtfully. 'It was a particularly gruesome murder, especially in a place as quiet as this.'

'I know…I read the newspapers from the archives in the library.' She gave a little shiver.

'Come on,' he said. 'Let's get what you need from next door so we can hit the sack. I don't know about you, but I'm bushed.'

Holly followed him back to the cottage next door and as quickly as she could she gathered a few bare essentials for the night and began to pack them into one of her cases.

Cameron watched her from the door of her bedroom where he was leaning. 'Do you really need such a big bag for one night?'

She looked up from what she was doing. 'I'm only bringing the basics.'

He left the door and came over and looked inside her bag. 'What are you bringing these for?' He held up her winter-weight pyjamas with pink baby elephants all over them.

She snatched them out of his hand and stuffed them back in the case. 'If you think I'm going to share a bed with you with less than two millimetres of fabric to cover me, think again.'

'You think I might make a move on you?'

Holly pursed her mouth at the twinkle of amusement in his blue-green eyes, not trusting herself to reply. What was he saying? That it was totally out of the question? That he wasn't the least bit attracted to her?

'Of course, if you'd like me to make a move on you I'd be more than happy to oblige,' he added with a sexy smile.

She closed her case with a little snap and, picking it up, shoved it towards him to carry, her eyes slipping away from his as his fingers brushed against hers.

'Holly, look at me,' he commanded gently.

She brought her eyes slowly back up to his, her stomach tilting at the darkening of his gaze as it held hers.

'I know this may surprise you, but for once I'm not joking,' he said.

Holly moistened her suddenly dry lips. 'Y-you're not?'

'No.'

'Oh…'

'Why do you find it so hard to believe I'm attracted to you?' he asked.

'We've only known each other such a short time…'

'That's true, but it doesn't take away from the fact that we've been firing sparks off each other from the very first moment we met. If that isn't full-on sexual chemistry I don't know what is.'

Holly had to look away from the sudden heat of his gaze. 'It doesn't mean we have to give in to such base impulses. We're both sensible adults with, one hopes, some measure of self-control.'

'Perhaps you'd better remind me of that in the middle of the night when you start to throw off those thermal pyjamas when it gets a little too hot in my bed,' he said with a wry grin as he opened the door for her to go through.

Holly didn't respond. She was already feeling a little too hot with him standing at least half a metre away. God only knew what it would be like sharing his bed for the night…

CHAPTER SEVENTEEN

IT WAS impossible to sleep with a man beside her who was snoring, Holly decided an hour or so later. Well, maybe not exactly snoring… It was more of a cute little snuffling sound but after the events of the evening she was far too restless to settle. She longed to straighten out her legs but Cameron had flung his limbs far and wide and she was on the very edge of the mattress as it was. And, as much as she hated admitting it, she also longed to rid herself of her thick pyjamas, which were starting to stick to her in all the wrong places.

She gave a frustrated sigh and squeezed her eyes shut, willing herself to sleep.

'Is everything all right?' Cameron asked, switching on the bedside lamp.

Holly nearly jumped out of her skin at the rich deep sound of his voice. She turned her head to see him looking down at her, his hair looking all mussed and sexy, his eyes still looking sleepy and his jaw peppered with dark stubble.

'You were snoring,' she said. 'You were keeping me awake.'

He gave a little frown. 'Really?'

'Well…it was more of a snuffle really but I'm a very light sleeper.'

'You should have elbowed me in the ribs.'

'I didn't want to wake you in case you…' She bit her lip to stop the rest spilling out.

'In case I what?'

Holly couldn't quite wrench her gaze from his. 'N-nothing.'

He reached out with a long finger and traced the upper curve of her mouth where some tiny beads of perspiration had gathered. 'You're hot.'

So are you, Holly replied mentally. *So hot I think I'm going to go up in flames if you come any closer with that sensual mouth of yours.*

'I did warn you about those pyjamas,' he said as he used the same finger to tuck one side of her damp hair behind her ear.

Holly could barely breathe. His eyes were holding hers like two powerful magnets, his naked chest so close to hers she could feel each breath he took—in and out, in and out…not quite touching her breasts as he exhaled but close enough to stir her senses into overdrive in case he did.

'Why are you looking at me like that?' he asked.

'How am I looking at you?'

'As if I'm going to kiss you.'

'That's ridiculous,' she said. 'As if you would be so…'

'So what?'

'Um…'

'Um?'

'Are you making a move on me?' she asked with a narrow-eyed look.

'Do you want me to make a move on you?'

'No! Of course not!'

He laughed, the deep rumble making his chest momentarily connect with hers. 'You're so cute when you're trying to hide what you're really feeling. Come on, admit it, Holly. Wouldn't you like to check out what's under my bonnet?'

'Why would I want to do that? I've seen plenty of naked men before. I'm sure you're no different.'

'I have a birthmark in a very interesting place. Do you want to look at it?'

She gave him a patronising look. 'That is the most pathetic line I've ever heard. Can't you think of something better than that?'

'I can, actually,' he said, drawing her even closer, his mouth coming down to hover just above hers. 'Want to hear it?'

Her mouth tingled from his breath moving over its too sensitive surface. Her heart was racing like a startled rabbit's, her quivering belly doing a complete somersault as his sea-green eyes turned to deep ocean-blue. She couldn't speak, didn't trust herself to speak. She was turning into a burning pool of longing and there was nothing she could do to stop it.

'I want to kiss you,' he said into the pulsing silence. 'In fact, I want to do a whole lot more than kiss you.'

'Y-you do?' she croaked as his head came closer and closer.

His mouth connected with hers in a kiss so soft she thought she must have imagined it. She ran her tongue over her lips to make sure and tasted him and her stomach gave another re-shuffle.

His mouth came back down and commandeered hers with such firm insistence that her heart rate escalated higher than her personal trainer had ever managed to achieve, notwithstanding his punishing workouts on the treadmill.

'God, you taste so good,' he said against her mouth, his tongue sweeping over its surface.

She gave a little groan as she felt its sexy rasp on

her tender skin. He deepened the kiss, pressing her back down on the bed as one of his hands slipped beneath her thick pyjama jacket to cup her right breast. She arched into his palm, relishing the feel of her nipple pressing into him with pert insistence.

He lifted his mouth from hers and, removing his hand from her breast, began undoing each of the little buttons on her jacket, one by one, his fingers brushing against her skin until she was trembling with need.

'I think we should take these off,' he said. 'What do you think?'

Holly was beyond thought, let alone speech, as he peeled away the thick pyjama jacket. He looked at her with eyes dark with desire before lowering his mouth to each breast, circling each areola with his tongue in ever decreasing circles until she was mad with the need to feel him take her in his mouth. He made her wait each time, her back almost lifting off the bed in delicious anticipation.

He left her breasts and began kissing his way down her stomach, pulling her pyjama trousers out of the way as he went. Holly sucked in her breath as he lingered over her belly button and then completely forgot to breathe when he went even lower.

Her fingers clutched at his head but it was impossible to control the tumultuous sensations as they flooded through her as his mouth worked its sensual magic. She felt herself lifting off and there was nothing she could do but go with each crashing wave of delicious sensation.

Once she'd come back to earth Holly felt his arm reach across her for the bedside drawer where he took out a small foil-wrapped packet.

Her eyes went wide as he kicked his boxer shorts out of the way before applying the condom. She couldn't see any sign of an interesting little birthmark anywhere, but what she could see was very impressive.

'We don't have to carry on if you don't want to,' he said, stroking one hand down her thigh.

'But that's not really fair…I mean…you…you made me …you know…'

'I know, but it doesn't mean you have to feel obliged in any way.'

Holly could hardly believe her ears. Here was a man who was prepared to put his needs aside, taking nothing that had happened so far for granted.

'But I want you to make love to me,' she said and then inwardly cringed at how desperate she'd sounded. 'I mean…if you want to, that is… I wouldn't want to force you or anything…you're probably not even all that attracted to me and you're only doing this because it's sort of expected that men will try and have sex with anyone, even when they don't feel a thing about—'

'Will you shut up?' he growled playfully, and pinned her with his body.

'I was only giving you an out…that's if you wanted…one…'

'I don't want an out,' he said, gently parting her thighs to accommodate him. 'I want an in.'

Holly gasped as he surged into her softness, going so deep she could feel him nudge against her womb. He began slowly, tantalisingly so, each thrust of his body sending a shockwave of delight through her before he increased his pace, his fullness sending her into a tailspin of feeling as her body gripped him tightly. She hadn't thought it possible to come again so quickly but with his body so thick and strong in hers and his fingers working their clever little magic where she most needed them she began to soar even higher than before.

She came floating back down in time to feel his body tense for his own freefall into paradise, the muscles of his back where her hands were pressed bunched in preparation.

He burst with a deep primal groan and her skin shivered all over in reaction at the sound of his pleasure, the pumping action of his body gradually slowing until he collapsed on top of her, his head buried against her neck.

Holly stroked her fingers up and down his back, a warm feeling of connection she'd never experienced before filling her. Julian would have been up and off her and in the shower by now, meticulously removing every trace of intimacy from his body, even brushing his teeth and rinsing with mouthwash.

Cameron was still encased in her body, his warm breath feathering against her neck as he drifted off to sleep.

'Cameron?' She gave him a little nudge.

'Mmm?' He gave a soft little sigh and nestled closer. His lips nuzzled her neck. 'You feel so nice…'

'Cameron.' She pushed at him. 'You can't fall asleep now!'

He propped himself up on one elbow to look at her. 'Why not?'

She frowned at him. 'Don't you want to have a shower or something?'

'What a great idea.' He eased himself away from her and discreetly disposed of the condom before tugging her out of bed by one hand.

'What are you doing?'

He pulled her into the bathroom with him. 'You

said you wanted a shower, didn't you? Let's save water and have it together.'

'I didn't mean together. I meant you—*ouch*!' She winced as the spray of water hit her. 'That's freezing!'

'I know, but we'll soon warm it up. Turn around and I'll scrub your back.'

Holly turned around but he didn't scrub her back. What he did was far more erotic. She could feel his growing thickness between her inner thighs, so excruciatingly close to where she most wanted him.

He turned her around and she opened her mouth for his kiss, the water cascading all around them somehow making everything she was feeling all the more intense.

Cameron tore his mouth off hers as he tried to get control. He hadn't brought a condom into the shower and he was ready to explode again. He sucked in a sharp little breath when she placed a flat hand on the middle of his chest and pushed him back against the shower stall. 'What are you doing?' he gasped.

She didn't answer. Instead she tiptoed her fingertips all the way down, gradually lowering her height until she was on her knees in front of him.

'Oh, dear God…' he groaned.

* * *

Holly woke just as dawn was breaking. She stretched languorously, amazed at how alive her body felt. Every part of her was still tingling in remembrance of the intimacy she and Cameron had shared.

She turned her head and saw him looking at her. It was hard to read his expression accurately but she wondered if he was regretting what had happened. There was a hint of a frown between his brows which seemed to suggest he was. Her heart instantly sank with disappointment. She had seen that look in Julian's eyes before and it had spelt the end of their relationship. What had she been thinking? That somehow things would be magically different with Cameron McCarrick? After all he was a full-blooded man who probably hadn't had a physical relationship since his break-up. No wonder he'd jumped at the chance she'd handed him on a plate, garnished lavishly with her naivety.

She lowered her eyes. 'You must think I'm totally without principles.'

'Why would I think that?'

'I haven't ever slept with someone I've only met a few days before.' She worried her bottom lip for a moment. 'I mean, we hardly even like each other and now we've…we've…'

'We've?'

'Become intimate.'

He laughed at her euphemistic choice of words. 'We had sex, Holly. And damn good sex, I might add.'

'But it mustn't happen again.'

'Oh? Why not?'

'Because…' she mentally cringed at his casual, unaffected tone '…because I don't want to complicate my life with a temporary affair. I'm only here for a year and it wouldn't be fair to you or indeed to me to get involved knowing it would all have to end eventually.'

Cameron inwardly frowned at her words. She wasn't ready for a relationship; it was clear she was still getting over her ex-fiancé—sleeping with him last night had more or less proved it. She wasn't the sleep-around type but perhaps wanted to prove something to herself—that she wasn't too afraid to get back on the horse, so to speak.

But the year had only just begun. There was time to make her change her mind if he played his cards right. What she needed right now was a friend and, although it would test his self-control to the very limits, he was determined to stand by her and help her gain more confidence. Her trust had been betrayed by her ex-fiancé but that didn't necessarily mean it couldn't be rebuilt with careful and tender handling. Anyone could see she had a big heart. She practically wore it on her sleeve, which made it all the easier to love her. He would just have to be patient.

'That's OK. I understand,' he said.

'I'm sorry, Cameron.' She eased herself out of the bed, taking the top sheet with her to cover herself. 'I hope I didn't mislead you in any way.'

'Not at all,' he answered in the same casual, easygoing tone. 'It was fun while it lasted.'

Holly wished he wasn't being so relaxed about it all. Why couldn't he be telling her how deeply she'd affected him last night instead of dismissing what had taken place as if it was of no real importance?

Because to him it is of no real importance, she reminded herself painfully. It was just sex.

Cameron got out of bed and stretched. 'Do you want the first shower?'

She looked away from his nakedness. 'No, you go right ahead. I think I'll go back to my place.'

'I'd better come with you.' He reached for his clothes.

'You don't need to bother.'

'It's no bother.' He zipped up his jeans. 'Aren't you going to get dressed?'

She looked down at the sheet she was wearing. 'Turn your back.'

He folded his arms across his chest. 'You're surely not serious?'

She lifted her chin. 'I am.'

He shook his head and turned around. 'What is it with women and modesty?' he said, addressing the wall in front of him.

'OK, I'm done,' she said a short time later.

He turned back around and, picking up her bag from the floor, led the way out without speaking another word.

When Holly arrived at the clinic that morning, she found that not one patient had booked in to see her.

Sally was neither surprised nor sympathetic. 'You have only yourself to blame. You can't expect to come to a town this size and tell people they're fat or someone's not guilty of murder when they've been tried and convicted. Nor can you insinuate that a well-respected, long-serving previous medical practitioner somehow made a mistake in a diagnosis, not to mention convince a teenage girl who's been viciously attacked not to press charges.'

'I did nothing of the sort!' Holly tried to defend herself at least on one point. 'Jacinta Jensen made that decision all by herself. I had absolutely nothing to do with it.'

Sally gave her a disbelieving look. 'You're supposed to be here to take the load off Dr

McCarrick but all you've done is make his life even busier. He's double-booked for the whole morning and half the afternoon, as well.'

Holly spun away in anger and stomped to her consulting room. She closed the door and leant back against it, fighting against tears of frustration.

She spent the morning reading journals but just before lunch Sally buzzed her on the intercom and informed her that she had a patient after all.

Holly went out to reception, her eyes widening slightly when she saw the name printed on the patient file. She turned to the waiting room and called, 'Mrs Lisa Shoreham?'

A frail-looking woman in her mid to late sixties got to her feet and, ignoring Holly's greeting, followed her to the consulting room.

Holly opened her mouth to ask her usual question when dealing with a new patient, but Mrs Shoreham got in first.

'I suppose you are wondering why I've come to see you.'

'Um…'

'But I had to come and tell you that I'm terribly sorry.' She looked down at her worn hands and turned her wedding ring over a few times.

Holly frowned in puzzlement. 'Sorry, for what?'

Lisa Shoreham brought her eyes back to hers. Holly had never seen such sadness in a woman's eyes before. Her entire face was like a road map of pain, fine lines of it etched in amongst deeper trenches of torment.

'It was my husband's idea...' Mrs Shoreham went on raggedly. 'He's never been the same since our daughter was...murdered...we both haven't...'

'I understand...' Holly said softly.

Mrs Shoreham looked down at her hands again. 'He's not well so you mustn't hold it against him. When we...lost Tina he started to drink. We both did for a while but I gave it up as I knew it wasn't going to bring her back. Nothing could ever do that. Grant couldn't handle the grief so he kept drinking to block it out.' Her eyes came back up. 'He hasn't seen a doctor for years, but I know he's not well. I guess that's why he did what he did...'

'What did he do?'

Mrs Shoreham started to cry, great wrenching sobs that tore at Holly's heart. 'He broke into your house and...' she said and dropped her head into her hands.

Holly was totally speechless. She stared at the sobbing woman, trying to get her head around this startling confession.

After a while the old woman lifted her head and looked at her through reddened eyes. 'He wanted to pay you back for defending Noel Maynard. We'd heard you weren't convinced he killed our daughter. I told him not to do such a thing but he wouldn't listen. He said you needed to be taught a lesson.'

'How did he get inside the house?'

'He had a key,' she said. 'The people who owned the cottages before Dr McCarrick bought them were our friends. We had each other's keys in case we ever lost a set as there's no locksmith around here.' She gave Holly a pleading look. 'I know you have every right to press charges but I beg you not to. It would kill him. He's not well.'

'I'm not going to press charges,' Holly assured her.

'Oh, thank you…' Mrs Shoreham started to sob anew. 'We've suffered enough… We can't take much more…It's just so hard with that…that… animal out of prison, walking around, while our daughter has been lying in the cemetery for the last twenty-five years.'

'It must be hell for you,' Holly said gently. 'I'm so sorry for causing you further pain by my actions and comments in regards to Mr Maynard.'

'It's all right,' Mrs Shoreham said. 'You weren't to know, being so new to town and all.' She gave her wedding ring another little twirl and added, 'I hope you weren't too upset by what you saw last night...'

'Not at all,' Holly lied. 'I kind of figured it was a practical joke and dismissed it as that.'

The older woman gave her a tremulous smile. 'You're being very gracious about this. Thank you.'

Holly smiled back. 'Thank you for coming to tell me. I know it must have been very hard for you under the circumstances.'

'I'd better be going...' Mrs Shoreham got to her feet. 'I don't like to leave Grant on his own too much...' She held out her hand. 'Thank you again for being so understanding.'

Holly took the thin hand in hers and gave it a gentle squeeze. 'Thank you, Mrs Shoreham.'

Cameron looked up from the paper when Holly came into the clinic kitchenette at lunch time. 'I heard you had a visit from Lisa Shoreham. How did it go?'

Holly pulled out a chair and flopped down into it. 'You're not going to believe this.'

'Try me.'

'Guess who broke into my house.'

'You've got to be kidding me.'

'Her husband did it to pay me back for doubting Noel Maynard's conviction.'

He whistled through his teeth as he absorbed the news. 'I didn't even know he came into town any more. I've heard he sits at home drinking himself into oblivion most days, not that you could blame him.'

Holly looked at the newspaper still in his hands. 'What does my star guide say today?'

He gave her a teasing look. 'You surely don't believe in all this rubbish, do you?'

She gave a non-committal shrug.

He turned to the paper and flicked through until he came to the horoscope section. '"Sagittarius: You will be confused about your feelings on a certain issue. Trust your heart and don't let other people's actions sway you from what you believe to be right."'

She gave him a sceptical glance. 'Now, what does yours say?'

He looked down at the paper once more. '"Gemini: You will be thinking of faraway places and lost loves…"' He let out a muttered curse as he tossed the paper to one side and got to his feet. 'God, who the hell writes this stuff?'

Holly swivelled in her chair to watch him as he strode

out of the room, his lunch abandoned on the table. She let out a tiny defeated sigh and, turning back, reached for one of the egg sandwiches off his plate.

CHAPTER EIGHTEEN

HOLLY decided that since no one had booked in to see her for the remainder of the day she would go for a drive to let off some steam. It was a beautiful day; the sun was warm but not overly hot so she opened her sun-roof and let the breeze lift her hair as she took the road for the hills behind Baronga Beach.

She was halfway along the dirt road leading to some caves she'd seen signposted a few kilometres back when she saw out of the corner of her eye a body lying on the side of the road, a crushed bicycle flung a few feet away.

She slammed on the brakes and reversed back, her heart beginning to race in panic.

Calm down, she mentally chanted. Think about trauma management principles. She got out of the car on shaking legs and inspected the body. There, crumpled into a broken heap, bleeding from multiple cuts and abrasions, his clothes torn and shredded, was Noel Maynard.

'Noel…' she gulped as she dropped to her knees beside him. 'What happened?'

Noel made some groaning sounds, but was clearly unconscious. He had a deep laceration running across his forehead from which blood was still running, his left femur was at a forty-five degree angle, his shirt was shredded, revealing multiple abrasions over the left chest, and the palms of his hands were white and, although she repeated his name several times, he made no verbal response.

Holly carefully shifted his position so that he was more on his side, protecting his airway from aspiration of vomit and mindful of protecting his neck from movement. She then retrieved her mobile phone from her handbag back at her car but, to her shock, there was no signal. She stared at her phone in horror. How could there be no signal? She looked around at the hills behind and let out a single expletive.

She turned and ran down the road until the signal came back. 'Oh, thank God!' She quickly keyed in Cameron's mobile number.

'McCarrick.'

'Cameron, it's Holly. I'm on the road out to Tolly's Caves. I've just come across Noel Maynard, about ten kilometres from town, I think. He's been knocked over and seriously injured. It looks like a hit-and-run.'

'Have you called the paramedics?'

'No, I called you first because I had to run down the road to pick up a signal as it is.'

'I'll come out right now with the paramedics. You say you're on the road to the caves—you must be on the back road. There's nothing out there. You're lucky to be in mobile range at all, so you can't be more than a few kilometres out. Hang on and we'll be there in ten or so minutes. Are you OK?'

'Yes, yes, I'm OK. But Noel is going to be lucky to survive this. Hurry up, Cameron. I've got my doctor's bag but it won't be enough. Please hurry,' she begged. 'I don't know if I can do this by myself.'

'Hang on, Holly, we're on our way.'

Holly grabbed her doctor's bag from the boot of her car. Even though she'd failed the practical exam of the Emergency Management of Severe Trauma course, one of the instructors had harangued the participants to take home from the course ideas on how they could apply the lessons to the situations in which they practised. He'd insisted that they all apply the EMST principles to putting together a doctor's bag of equipment to allow them to deal with the basics of ABCDE.

As Holly hurried back to Noel's side she was silently grateful that she had at least taken that much on board. Now her trauma skills were going to be sorely tested and this was no practice scenario in an air-conditioned educational centre. It was the real thing, in the dirt and grime of the roadside, with no help and limited equipment.

She pulled open her bag and put on a pair of gloves and some goggles. She then took her only adult Guedel's airway and inserted it into Noel's mouth. He was still breathing spontaneously but had stopped groaning, becoming more deeply unconscious. She had no oxygen supply, no bag or mask. If he stopped breathing, the best she could do was use a plastic air viva respirator tube to do protected assisted respiration. She desperately hoped it wouldn't come to that.

She took her stethoscope and listened to his chest. There were no breath sounds over the left chest, which was covered with abrasions, presumably from where he had been dragged along the road by whichever vehicle had knocked him down. She felt his chest and noted crepitus over the left upper chest, indicating subcutaneous emphysema. Percussion was hyper-resonant over the left chest and his trachea was shifted to the right, the hallmarks of a left tension pneumothorax. His hands were pale and sweaty, clearly signs of hypovolaemic shock, and possibly cardiogenic shock as a result of the pneumothorax.

Holly had some large bore IV canulae in her kit. She cleared away what was left of Noel's shirt from the front of his chest, took an alcohol swab and prepped the second left intercostal space in the mid-clavicular line. She punctured the skin with the canula over the top of the second rib, slowly advancing it until it suddenly gave way as she punctured the pleura. There was a distinct hiss of air as the high pressure pneumothorax decompressed. She then inserted another canula next to the first, to increase the air flow. Noel's breathing seemed to improve and he was moaning again. Holly listened to the left chest again with her stethoscope—this time there was at least some air entry to hear.

In her kit there was one bag of normal saline and a giving set. She connected the set to the bag of fluid and ran through some saline to flush the line. She took an elastic tourniquet and applied it to Noel's left mid-forearm. She then took another alcohol swab and prepped over a large vein on the radial side of Noel's left wrist, inserting her only remaining IV canula into the vein successfully. She attached the giving set, removed the tourniquet and started running in the normal saline full bore.

She had a few four-inch crêpe bandages in her kit, which was now looking a little depleted. She removed the cellophane outer covering from one of the bandages and carefully applied a head bandage, trying to move Noel's neck as little as possible, but successfully controlling the bleeding from his forehead. She then took a pair of scissors and cut open his trousers over the angled left leg. He clearly had a fractured femur. His left shoe was missing and he had no socks on. Holly felt for his dorsalis pedis pulse—it was absent and the sole of his foot appeared dusky.

The arterial supply is blocked at the fracture site, she thought.

As gently as she could, she straightened the thigh, causing an enhanced bout of moaning from Noel. Holly noted that the peripheral pulses in the left foot were now palpable. Looking around, she noticed a piece of pipe lying close by. She retrieved it and found a reasonably straight piece of stick. Using these as temporary splints and her remaining two crêpe bandages, she roughly splinted Noel's left thigh, again checking that his peripheral foot pulses were intact.

She looked in her bag. There was little else. She took a small penlight torch and checked Noel's pupils. The left pupil was dilated and unreactive, the right normal-sized and reactive.

He could have intracranial haemorrhage, Holly thought. *But there's nothing I can do about that here.*

Just then a familiar city sound wafted in from the distance—the sound of a wailing siren. Holly breathed a sigh of relief. Thank God, the cavalry had arrived and Noel was still alive.

Within a few seconds a red-and-white country ambulance pulled in front of Holly's car, Cameron the first to jump out.

Cameron quickly took in Noel Maynard's shattered form, but with tubes and bandages attached and a white-faced Holly beside him, her doctor's bag looking almost empty.

'You OK?' he asked.

She gave a quick nod.

'What's your assessment of his injuries?'

'He's got a GCS about seven or eight, responding with groans to pain. There's a bleeding laceration on his forehead, which I've controlled with a bandage. His airway's clear and he's breathing spontaneously. He's got a dilated non-reacting left pupil—my worry is an intracranial haemorrhage. He's got left fractured ribs and subcutaneous emphysema, and had no breath sounds on the left and a deviated trachea to the right, so he had a left tension. I decompressed that with a couple of large-bore IV needles, but he's going to need a definitive chest drain. I started my only bag of saline through the largest bore IV canula I had, about a fourteen gauge, I think. I'm running it in full bore and it's almost finished. And he's got a fractured left femur, which I've roughly splinted. It had been angled and there were no peripheral foot pulses; they've come back since I've straightened the leg and splinted it the best way I could.'

'That's the most impressive roadside resuscitation I've ever seen,' said Cameron, directing the paramedics with their trolley to the patient. 'I have to say I am very impressed. Well done. Listen, can you stabilize his neck while I get a hard collar on?'

'Sure.' Holly could feel a warm inward glow at his praise. She'd been so worried she wouldn't cope and yet here he was telling her what a good job she'd done.

Soon the collar was applied, some oxygen was running via a mask, more IV fluids were attached and Noel was log-rolled and carefully placed on to a spine board.

'I'll go back in the ambulance with him, Holly. You follow in your car. We'll radio through for a retrieval team from St George by air ambulance. Will you be OK to drive?'

'Sure. I'm fine,' she said, doing her best to disguise her shaking limbs as the stress of her encounter started to hit home.

Within seconds the back of the ambulance was closed and it moved off down the road, lights flicking red and siren wailing.

Holly slumped into the driver's seat of her car and stared straight ahead, taking several deep breaths before turning the ignition and starting her engine.

Once the airlift team had taken Noel Maynard to the nearest trauma centre, Cameron turned to Rob Aldridge, who had not long come back from the accident site to talk to Holly.

'Any idea who's responsible?' Rob asked.

'No idea at all,' Holly said. 'I didn't see a single vehicle on my drive out there.'

'With the sort of injuries he's got, the car that hit him must have some sort of damage,' Cameron pointed out. 'Noel's bike is a mess.'

'Yes…' Rob rubbed his chin thoughtfully. 'I wonder if it's the same person who trashed your cottage.'

Holly exchanged a quick glance with Cameron.

'The person responsible for that has already come forward and apologised,' she said. 'I don't want to take it any further.'

'Who did it?'

'I don't think that's—'

'Grant Shoreham,' Cameron said, earning a caustic look from Holly.

Rob rolled his lips inward. 'I'd better go and have a chat with him after I've spoken to Maynard's mother.'

'I can go and see her if you like,' Holly offered.

'No,' Rob said. 'I need to get a statement from her about Noel's exacts movements.'

Holly waited until the police officer had left before turning on Cameron. 'I promised Mrs Shoreham I wouldn't report that stupid chicken incident—now you've gone and blabbed.'

Cameron looked down at her. 'You've got dust on your nose.'

'I've got...what?' She put her hand up to her face.

'And you need to go home and have a shower and take the rest of the day off.'

Holly wanted to argue with him on principle but the truth was she didn't have the energy to do it. 'Fine. I'll go home. I don't have any patients, anyway.'

Cameron watched her stalk off, a small frown beginning to pull his brows together as some thoughts shifted around in his head. He turned around after a moment and reached for the phone and dialled Accident and Emergency at St George and asked to be put through to the doctor on duty. After he'd introduced himself, he asked the doctor to conduct several blood tests on Noel Maynard, who was due to arrive shortly.

'Wilson's disease?' the registrar asked. 'What's that got to do with his trauma? I've never seen a case.'

'It is rare. But it could be important in this case. How soon can you get the results?'

'God, I don't know. I've never ordered the test. Listen, Biochem here is pretty good. I'd be surprised if it would take more than a few hours. I'll see if I can fast-track it.'

'Good, thanks for that. Can you fax the results to our clinic here as soon as you get them through? Here's the number…'

CHAPTER NINETEEN

HOLLY had not long showered and changed when she heard a tentative knock on her front door. She peered through the curtains to see who it was before opening the door to Jacinta Jensen.

'Dr Saxby…can I talk to you?'

'Sure.' Holly closed the door once she was inside. 'How are you?'

Jacinta lowered her eyes. 'I'm fine…'

'Would you like a glass of juice or something?' Holly asked. 'I was just about to have one.'

'No…no, I just want to get this over with…' She twisted her hands together.

Holly frowned. 'Why don't you sit down and tell me what's on your mind?' She led the way to the sofa and watched as Jacinta perched on the edge of it while she took the chair opposite.

'Do your mother and stepfather know you are here?'

The young girl shook her head, her eyes downcast.

'Have you changed your mind about pressing charges?' Holly asked after a long silence.

Jacinta looked up at her. 'He didn't do it.'

Holly stared at her for a moment. 'What do you mean?'

'Noel Maynard didn't do it,' Jacinta said. 'I only said he did because I…I…' She began to cry.

Holly left her chair to sit on the sofa by the young girl's side, taking her hand in hers and stroking it. 'If he didn't do it to you, then who did?'

Jacinta looked at her with red-rimmed eyes. 'My stepbrother, Martin.'

Holly tried to hide her shock but it was almost impossible.

'It's not really his fault,' Jacinta continued. 'I've been awful to him for ages. He ignores me most of the time but this time I…I…made him so angry he grabbed me and gave me a little shake. I bumped my eye on his wardrobe.'

'What were you doing in his bedroom?' Holly asked after another little silence.

Jacinta's face coloured up. 'I know you're going to think this is terrible of me, but I wanted him to sleep with me. I tried to get him to kiss me but he wouldn't… That's why I came to you for the pill. I think I'm in love with him.' She gave Holly an agonised look. 'Is that against the law or some-thing?'

Holly let out a little sigh. 'It won't be against the law when you're a little older but right now you're under age.'

'My mother will be so ashamed of me,' Jacinta sobbed. 'I'll be sent away to boarding school for this, I just know it. I hate myself. I don't know why I behave the way I do… It's just I still really miss my Dad and I can't quite forgive my Mum for finding someone else so soon. Do you think I'm bad?'

'Of course I don't. I know it's a little different, but when my parents separated they both had new partners within a few short weeks. I was furious with both of them.'

Jacinta dabbed at her eyes with the tissue Holly had handed her. 'I hated changing schools and I have no friends. No one likes me here.'

You and me, too, honey, Holly thought. 'It takes time to make friends in a new place,' she said. 'You have to build up trust, but also you have to learn to like yourself more. That way others will see the real you instead of the façade you put up. Give it more time; you'll settle in eventually.'

'Thanks,' Jacinta said. 'I just had to tell someone. Martin will be furious; he made me promise but I heard Mr Maynard got hit by a car… I was so frightened that…that…someone might have done that to him because of what I'd said.'

Holly frowned at the possibility of someone, perhaps Jacinta's stepfather, taking vigilante action. He wouldn't be the only possibility, though; there were plenty of people in town who wanted to see Noel Maynard dead or gone.

'Come on.' Holly picked up her car keys. 'I'll give you a lift home. You'd better have some back-up while you tell your folks the truth. Might as well be me.'

'You sure you don't mind?'

'Not at all,' Holly said. 'I've got nothing else planned.'

It wasn't a pleasant scene at the Jensens' when Jacinta dropped her bombshell. Holly hated every minute of it but she stuck it out for the teenager's sake, finally extricating herself once the shouting and recriminations had died down. Instead of returning to the cottage, she took the road to Betty Maynard's. She couldn't help wondering how the poor old woman was dealing with the news of her son's serious injuries.

When she drove up over the ridge that led to the old house she saw that another car was parked outside, an old-model beaten up Ford that looked as if it had gone around the clock a few times.

Holly went to the door and knocked, but no one answered. She pressed her ear to the door to listen for any sound of movement inside but it was eerily quiet. She looked down at the rusty doorknob. Should she go in? What if the old lady had fallen or even had a heart attack in shock at the news of her son's accident?

She turned the handle and opened the door a crack. 'Mrs Maynard? It's me, Holly Saxby. Are you all right?'

'There's no one home,' a voice said from behind her on the veranda.

Holly swung around to see a man in his late sixties standing in the bright sunlight, a pair of sunglasses shielding his eyes. He looked vaguely familiar but she couldn't quite place him. 'I'm sorry... Do I know you?' she asked.

'You met my wife this morning.'

Grant Shoreham was twenty-five years older than the photographs she'd seen of him and Lisa in the newspaper articles documenting their daughter's death, but no wonder she'd thought he was familiar.

Holly hesitated over offering him her hand and introducing herself formally. He looked uncomfortable in her presence as it was, no doubt because of last night's incident, if not because of the rumours he'd heard about her regarding his daughter's murderer. The pain on his face was evident in spite of the heavily tinted sunglasses. His whole body seemed to be almost bent double with it, the grief of the years weighing him down.

'Mr Shoreham…' she began awkwardly. 'I hope you'll forgive me for causing you and your wife any hurt… I was just confused over some results that came in… I wanted to make sure everything was—'

'I thought you'd come here,' he said, cutting her off, his voice shaking with emotion. 'I knew you'd come to see the old lady but you're too late.'

Holly felt her stomach tilt sideways. 'W-what do you mean I'm too late? Has something happened to her?'

He didn't answer; instead he stepped out of the sun and made his way past her on the veranda to enter the house.

She turned and followed him inside. 'Mr Shoreham?'

He reached for the back of a chair with one shaking hand to steady himself as he faced her, his face pinched with sadness. 'You shouldn't have come to Baronga Beach. We were finally starting to put our lives together and now you've torn them apart.'

'I'm sorry…'

'You don't understand how it's been,' he went on as if she hadn't spoken. 'For years I've tried to forget but it just won't go away.'

'I understand…' Holly inserted softly.

He suddenly slammed his hand on the worn table, his expression darkening with anger. 'How can you possibly understand?'

'I—I understand you've suffered terribly in the loss of your daughter,' she said, trying to soothe him, but he became even more agitated.

'The loss?' He almost spat the words at her. 'She wasn't lost like a sock in the wash. She was murdered.'

Holly swallowed nervously. 'Y-yes…I mean your daughter's murder.'

He gave a cracked bark of odd-sounding laughter and Holly wondered if he was on the edge of a complete breakdown. He certainly was acting like it. His movements were jerky and agitated and she imagined his eyes behind those dark glasses were shifting all over the place as he tried to hold himself together.

'I really don't want to do this…' he said after a tight silence, his voice breaking on the words. 'My wife likes you…she says you're just what this place needs, but I can't let you do this to us. Not now. Not after all we've been through.'

Holly stared at him, trying to make sense of his words. She was about to ask him what he meant when, to her absolute horror, he reached for a knife that was lying on the bench closest to him and came stumbling towards her.

She stepped backwards in shock but tripped over the worn linoleum on the floor at the door. She cracked her head on one of the legs of the table but somehow managed to escape the first stab of the knife as it lunged towards her. She rolled away and pushed one of the rickety chairs at him but he was still coming. Fear filled her throat until she could hardly breathe and her stomach threatened to liquefy in panic.

'Why are you doing this?' she gasped, blocking him with the table. She was cornered now but at least he'd have to climb on the table to get her. She tried to reassure herself that he looked too frail and sickly to be able to do that but she wasn't prepared to take any chances.

'You've left me no choice,' he said, looking for a way to get to her. 'You've ruined everything, don't you see? You're making people doubt and I'm not having that. Not after all this time, not after all we've suffered.'

'Please, Mr Shoreham, let's talk about this like sensible adults. Put down the knife…please. I know you don't really want to hurt me. Your wife told me you only did the chicken thing to scare me. I know you're sorry. It's all right. I'm not going to press charges.'

'Put the knife down, Grant,' Cameron said from the door.

Holly almost collapsed in relief and would have fallen to the floor if the table hadn't been in the way.

Grant Shoreham turned and faced Cameron, the knife still in his hand. 'Don't make me kill you as well, Dr McCarrick. Lisa would never forgive me if I had to do that.'

'She's not going to forgive you anyway, is she, Grant?' Cameron asked.

Holly held her breath against the tension in the small, dark, dusty room.

'You killed Tina, didn't you?' Cameron went on in the same calm, even tone.

Holly watched as Grant Shoreham began to crumple, the knife slipping from his hand to drop at his feet.

'I didn't mean to do it…' The old man's sobs were heart-wrenching as he put his head in his hands. 'She was disobeying my orders by continuing to see that filthy Maynard boy. I followed her here… I was going to threaten Maynard with the knife. When I put my hands around her neck to stop her from shouting out to warn Maynard she grabbed it out of my pocket… I tried to grab it but she twisted around… It went so deep into her stomach I panicked. She was dead before I could go for help… Lisa can't ever find out I did it…'

'So you let an innocent man go to jail for a murder he didn't commit?' Holly finally found her voice.

He gave a miserable nod. 'I had to… There was no other choice… Then Maynard confessed… God knows why.' He sank to the nearest chair and started shaking. 'I ran him down on the back road. I had to stop people finding out… If he was dead it would all go away again. I had to make it all go away again…I had to…'

Cameron picked up the knife from the floor and secured it before coming over to where the old man was seated. 'The blood that connected Maynard to your daughter wasn't his, was it, Grant?'

He shook his head and continued to quietly sob.

'That's why you haven't been to see Dr Cooper since your daughter's death. Or me, for the past four years. You've refused to come in for a check-up even though your health has been pretty obviously deteriorating,' Cameron continued.

Grant nodded again, the tears streaming unheeded down his face.

Holly watched as Cameron took the sunglasses off

the old man's face and looked into his eyes. Even from her cramped spot behind the table she could see the telltale copper-coloured Kaiser-Fleischer rings in his eyes. Wilson's disease.

'Where's Betty Maynard?' Cameron asked the slumped figure in the chair.

'In the boot of my car...tied up...I was going to torch it.'

Cameron took out his mobile and pressed rapid-dial for Rob and an ambulance, his eyes going to Holly's.

Holly listened as he relayed the situation, her heart chugging with the aftershock of fear at what could have been her fate if Cameron hadn't put the pieces of the puzzle together in time.

It seemed an age before the ambulance and Rob arrived, but finally it was over. A traumatized Betty was taken away in the ambulance and Grant Shoreham was taken into custody.

'I'll organise for someone to collect your car later,' Cameron said as he led Holly to his four-wheel drive vehicle. 'You're in no fit state to drive.'

'How did you figure it out?' She turned in her seat to look at him once they were on their way.

'Don't go giving me the credit, sweetheart,' he said. 'You were the one who set the ball in motion. I just started to see a pattern in the way that ball was bouncing, that's all.' He gave her a quick glance. 'I had a phone call from Clinton Jensen, who told me Jacinta had confessed to you that it hadn't been Noel who'd attacked her. For a time there I was starting to think Clinton might've taken the law into his own hands. But then I wondered if it might have been Geoffrey Cooper. He seemed to be overreacting to the news of your visit to his father. I think we'll find that Neville Cooper had discovered his mistake over the diagnosis he made but before he could do anything about it he had a stroke. That would explain why he was so upset at your questions about Noel and his treatment. He would've heard Noel had been released but in his state of health he had no way of destroying the records.'

'Do you think Geoffrey Cooper knew anything about it?'

'I'm not sure. I don't like the guy that much, but that's for more personal reasons.'

'Oh?' She turned to look at him again.

'Yeah,' he said with a smile. 'How dare he ask my girl out for a drink and then stand her up?'

Holly swallowed. 'Your girl?'

'That's if you want to be, of course,' he added as he pulled into his driveway.

She waited until he came around to her side to help

her out before asking, 'And how long do you want me to be your… your girl?'

'To tell you the truth, sweetheart, I would much prefer you to be my wife, but since I've only known you, what is it now…five days, I thought you might think I was stark raving mad for proposing so soon.'

Holly blinked. 'Y-your wife?'

'I love you, Holly. I love everything about you. I love the way you told me off for overtaking you that first day. I think that might be when I first fell in love with you, or maybe it was when I pulled you out of the water at the beach with your hair all sandy and your make-up running. You looked so cute. I love that you defended a man everyone had written off as guilty. I love that you care for your patients with your whole heart and I love the way you are smiling at me right now. Does it mean what I think it means?'

'What do you think it means?'

He gathered her into his arms and lowered his head to hers. 'I could be wrong, but I think you might have just agreed to marry me. Am I right?'

Holly pressed her lips to his in a hot little kiss. She looked into his eyes and smiled. 'You are most definitely right, Dr McCarrick.'

EPILOGUE

THE whole town seemed to be there for the wedding three months later. Holly could see all the familiar smiling faces as she came up the aisle on her father's arm towards Cameron, who, dressed in a suit, looked breathtakingly handsome. Noel Maynard, still on crutches, and Harry Winston, his two groomsmen, were standing somewhat nervously by his side.

Holly's eyes went to Jacinta Jensen and Belinda Proctor, who were acting as assistants to her bridesmaids, her friends from Medical School, Annabelle and Jodie.

Her mother was dabbing at tears next to Betty Maynard, who was grinning from ear to ear, her daughter Nell standing by her side. Cameron's sister Freya was winking at her mischievously from the row in front and even Major Dixon was standing there next to Rob Aldridge, his back ramrod straight, his hand lifted in a salute as she went past.

Holly's gaze went to where Cameron's parents were standing in the pew at the front, holding hands, their love for each other, in spite of the tragedy they'd faced all those years ago, clear for all to see.

Her heart felt too big for her chest as she took her place by Cameron's side, his hand reaching for hers and giving it a little squeeze.

He leaned down to whisper in her ear. 'You'll never guess what my horoscope is for today.'

Holly gave him a twinkling little smile. 'You're surely not going to read it to me now?'

He grinned at her. 'I memorised it just for you.'

She did her best not to giggle but hardly a day went past when he didn't make her laugh. How she loved him for that!

'Go on, then,' she whispered back. 'What did it say?'

'"Gemini: you have good stars for love and romance, perhaps a wedding or family celebration is in the air." Not bad, huh?'

'Guess what mine said.'

'Go on, tell me.'

'"Sagittarius: there are interesting stars around you at present. Could it be there is a very special announcement to be made, something to do with a pregnancy, perhaps?"'

'Are you serious?' His eyes grew dark with emotion.

'You know me, darling.' She put his hand on her still flat abdomen and smiled up at him. 'I'm always serious.'

MEDICAL ROMANCE™

Large Print

Titles for the next six months…

April

RESCUE AT CRADLE LAKE	Marion Lennox
A NIGHT TO REMEMBER	Jennifer Taylor
THE DOCTORS' NEW-FOUND FAMILY	
	Laura MacDonald
HER VERY SPECIAL CONSULTANT	Joanna Neil
A SURGEON, A MIDWIFE: A FAMILY	Gill Sanderson
THE ITALIAN DOCTOR'S BRIDE	Margaret McDonagh

May

THE CHRISTMAS MARRIAGE RESCUE	Sarah Morgan
THEIR CHRISTMAS DREAM COME TRUE	Kate Hardy
A MOTHER IN THE MAKING	Emily Forbes
THE DOCTOR'S CHRISTMAS PROPOSAL	Laura Iding
HER MIRACLE BABY	Fiona Lowe
THE DOCTOR'S LONGED-FOR BRIDE	Judy Campbell

June

THE MIDWIFE'S CHRISTMAS MIRACLE	Sarah Morgan
ONE NIGHT TO WED	Alison Roberts
A VERY SPECIAL PROPOSAL	Josie Metcalfe
THE SURGEON'S MEANT-TO-BE BRIDE	Amy Andrews
A FATHER BY CHRISTMAS	Meredith Webber
A MOTHER FOR HIS BABY	Leah Martyn

MILLS & BOON®

Live the emotion

0307 LP 2P P1 Medical

MEDICAL ROMANCE™

 *Large Print*

July

THE SURGEON'S MIRACLE BABY — Carol Marinelli
A CONSULTANT CLAIMS HIS BRIDE — Maggie Kingsley
THE WOMAN HE'S BEEN WAITING FOR
— Jennifer Taylor
THE VILLAGE DOCTOR'S MARRIAGE — Abigail Gordon
IN HER BOSS'S SPECIAL CARE — Melanie Milburne
THE SURGEON'S COURAGEOUS BRIDE — Lucy Clark

August

A WIFE AND CHILD TO CHERISH — Caroline Anderson
THE SURGEON'S FAMILY MIRACLE — Marion Lennox
A FAMILY TO COME HOME TO — Josie Metcalfe
THE LONDON CONSULTANT'S RESCUE — Joanna Neil
THE DOCTOR'S BABY SURPRISE — Gill Sanderson
THE SPANISH DOCTOR'S CONVENIENT BRIDE
— Meredith Webber

September

A FATHER BEYOND COMPARE — Alison Roberts
AN UNEXPECTED PROPOSAL — Amy Andrews
SHEIKH SURGEON, SURPRISE BRIDE — Josie Metcalfe
THE SURGEON'S CHOSEN WIFE — Fiona Lowe
A DOCTOR WORTH WAITING FOR — Margaret McDonagh
HER L.A. KNIGHT — Lynne Marshall

MILLS & BOON®
Live the emotion

0307 LP 2P P2 Medical